Beguiled

Julia Keaton

NCP

Be sure to check out our website for the very best in fiction at fantastic prices!

When you visit our webpage, you can:

* Read excerpts of currently available books
* View cover art of upcoming books and current releases
* Find out more about the talented artists who capture the magic of the writer's imagination on the covers
* Order books from our backlist
* Find out the latest NCP and author news--including any upcoming booksignings by your favorite NCP author
* Read author bios and reviews of our books
* Get NCP submission guidelines
* And so much more!

We offer a 20% discount on all new ebook releases!
(Sorry, but short stories are not included in this offer.)

We also have contests and sales regularly, so be sure to visit our webpage to find the best deals in ebooks and paperbacks! To find out about our new releases as soon as they are available, please be sure to sign up for our newsletter!

The newsletter is available by double opt in only and our customer information is never shared!

Visit our webpage at:
www.newconceptspublishing.com

New Concepts Publishing
5202 Humphreys Rd.
Lake Park, GA 31636

ISBN 1-58608-667-7
Beguiled (c) copyright February 2004 by Julia Keaton

Cover art (c) copyright 2004 Eliza Black

NCP books are available at special quantity discounts for bulk purchases for sales promotions, premiums, fund raising, or educational use. For details, write, email, or phone New Concepts Publishing, 5202Humphreys Rd., Lake Park, GA 31636, ncp@newconceptspublishing.com, Ph. 229-257-0367, Fax 229-219-1097.

First NCP Paperback Printing: November 2004
10 9 8 7 6 5 4 3 2 1

Printed in the United States of America

Dedication:

To my mother, who is always my inspiration and my rock. I would be nothing without her.

Beguiled

Julia Keaton

Historical Romance

New Concepts   Georgia

Chapter One

The middle of nowhere (England/Scotland border) 1540

"Unhand me you goatish, fly-bitten canker-blossom!"

The outlandish words echoed over the countryside like the voice of god. Startled birds scrambled in flight with a rush of wings to escape it. The forest fell eerily silent at their passing, still as a tomb.

The echo stunned Alexandra from her self-absorption, her dilemma briefly forgotten. Quiet roared in her ears. Frigid wind whipped her cape out like a sail, fallen leaves blowing like a vortex around her horse's legs. She froze, listening for the broach of peace again, hope burgeoning in her chest. She'd thought herself utterly, completely alone, never to see another soul for all eternity.

7

Oaks, birches, and other trees she had no name for boxed her in, leaves burnished in flame and gold. If she hadn't been in such trouble, she would have thought it quite beautiful. The ground was relatively smooth underneath the tangling brush that obscured her passage—and which way she'd come. The forest was as thick and impenetrable as the king's army. She knew this—had been roaming the land for an eternity, looking for a way out. If she hadn't fallen asleep and her horse hadn't had a mind of his own—

A fearful cry filtered through the trees. She jumped in the saddle like she'd been goosed. Closer this time, its direction more distinct as she moved through the woods. From the West? She wondered. Shielding her eyes from the setting sun, she strained her senses in her search. The voice had to be coming from there. She thanked god for blessing the stranger with powerful lungs.

Alex nudged her horse, Firedancer, forward, her decision made. Low limbs snapped like the crack of a whip with their passing, twigs and dried leaves crunching underfoot. The noise, deafening to her ears, made Alex cringe and grit her teeth in anxiety. Though she had no cause for quiet other than safety's sake, she felt until she had assessed the situation that caution was best.

Certes—she wanted no part of what was ahead.

They had gone only a short distance when the trees began to thin. Broken stumps rotting in the ground were evidence of man's progress. Alex could just make out the clearing of the road. She had been so close all this time.

As she neared, the human presence became more discernible. Movement caught her attention, a flurry of color, but she dared not reveal herself.

A woman shrieked suddenly like a cat thrown in water. Alex grimaced at the sound.

"Oy! Giver over, luv!" a man yelled.

Ah, so it was a lover's quarrel. She shook her head in disgust. How a man could say such to a screaming shrew was beyond Alex's grasp. And to think, she would soon subjugate herself to such games.... A heavy sigh escaped her. If only Grandfather hadn't left her, she wouldn't be in this predicament now. She cleared her head of her woe, determined to face the here and now.

'Twould be uncomfortable interrupting their tryst, but she need be on her way. Alex nudged Firedancer onward.

"I say again, release my purse, brigand!"

Alex halted, stunned. What ho! A thief? Heroics were completely out of her depth. She gazed longingly to where she knew the road to be, debating what to do.

Why could the chit not just hand over her coin and let the man be?

A second ticked by. Firedancer twitched in nervousness, mirroring her emotions. A bead of sweat crept down her neck, and she wiped at it with her shoulder.

The girl obviously needed help, and there was no one else around ... Alex would charge the thief. Perhaps that would frighten him off. And if not

... well, she could keep going. She nodded in satisfaction. Aye, 'twas a good plan.

Withdrawing her rapier for effect, Alex dug her heels into her horse's flanks before she could change her mind. Firedancer leapt into eager action, plunging through the short distance of forest. Low branches tore at her head and arms, filling her mouth with leaves. She spat and sputtered, clinging for dear life to the saddle, praying she wouldn't be scraped off on one of the trunks. What insanity had possessed her to keep such a flighty animal?

Firedancer vaulted into the air and over a bush like he'd sprouted wings. The gauntlet was clear— except for a man and woman standing stock still in the road.

The girl was the only one to react, flinging herself from Alex's path of doom. A strangled battle cry erupted from Alex's throat.

She swung mightily at the mammoth of a man, her victory imminent, missing him by an arm's length as the blade sailed safely through the air and out of her grasp.

Firedancer, a war-horse who never missed his chance for glory, ground to an immediate halt, slamming her into his head as he rear kicked the thief. Bright lights danced before her eyes, and she blinked rapidly to disperse them. She whirled around, horrified to see him crumpled in a heap.

"What have you done?!" Alex whispered furiously at Firedancer, rubbing the knot welling upon her forehead, thinking frantically of the implication of murder. She jumped off and stumbled, then hobbled like an old woman to the man. Poking him cautiously with her toe, she was gratified to hear him moan in pain.

"He still lives you foul-tempered horse." Looking him over, she saw his head looked to be bumped mighty hard, and the girl had taken the hide off his bones with her claws, but he would live.

Everything had worked out according to plan.

The girl sobbed from across the road, drawing her attention, looking upon Alex with a woebegone expression. 'Twas difficult for her to believe she'd stood up against such a giant of a man. Either the girl was lightminded or ... or ... well, the girl was lightminded. She could think of no reason why she would have done such a foolhardy thing.

Shrugging, Alex withdrew a length of braided leather from a pouch at her waist. 'Twill do the job well, she thought.

Crouching low to the ground, her eyes watered at the unwashed smell of thug. Holding her breath, she put her shoulder against his back and pushed ... and pushed. Straining every muscle, forced to breathe the foul air, she finally managed to roll him onto his stomach. She stood, panting from her exertion. He hadn't looked that heavy. She wrestled his beefy arms to his back and bound them together. Satisfied he could cause no more hurt for a time, she turned to leave.

Somehow, the distraught girl had come skidding across the dirt into Alex's 'waiting' arms.

Between reverent, hurried kisses on Alex's face

11

and neck, she murmured, "I thank thee, kind Sir. You are my hero ... my Savior!"

Sputtering, Alex pushed her away and held her at bay with one hand, frantically checking her mustache with the other. She sighed, relieved as she felt its comforting presence. The paste was hard put to stand up to such rigors.

The girl began thoroughly covering her knuckles and palm with affection. Alex snatched her hand back like she'd taken a bite out and hugged it to her breast. "Madam! I pray thee, we must remember propriety above all else!"

Subdued for a moment, the girl raised her worshipful gaze to Alex's horrified one. It seemed she had somehow managed to make a conquest of the lady—using the term loosely. Dusty black hair hung in straggled locks down to her waist. Her face was covered with grime and a few tear tracks, but cleaned up, she would be a lovely girl. She had the look of a cat to her—a wildcat—with her arched brows and amber eyes.

Alex desperately needed to be away. She had enough complication in her life, she needed not one more.

"W-what is your name, Madam?" She moved casually closer to her horse.

The girl chuckled and smiled coyly—as though they were not standing in the middle of nowhere beside a trussed ruffian. "Forgive me, kind Sir. I do but forget my manners." She curtsied deeply. "I am Constance Blackmore. My father is Lord Derwin."

Saints! She never would have imagined....

What sort of father let his child roam the country-side unescorted?

Playing her part, Alex removed her plumed cap and made a sweeping bow. She thought it wise to forego kissing the maiden's hand. "Lord Alex Montague at your service. Protector of the innocent, righter of injustice." She rather liked the way that sounded, and it was well worth the prick of guilt she felt at her deception.

Lady Constance twittered. Alex smiled nervously, eyeing her horse, wondering if she ought not to have encouraged the girl.

"Perchance we shall meet again, milady. If it pleases you, I must be away. The hour grows late."

"It most certainly does not please me. I wouldst have you see me home to my father. He will be very worried."

"I cannot, forgive me." She climbed onto her horse. "'Tis near full dark, and I must find shelter for the night." She did not like the dark. There was too great a chance she'd injure herself—or rather, Firedancer would injure her.

Constance clung to her leg. Alex resisted her first impulse to shake her off like an annoying pup.

"You can stay at Derwin Hall." She batted her lashes beguilingly. When Alex made no response, she said, "You cannot leave me here. What sort of gentleman are you?"

"Saints! I cannot go traipsing about the country-side. I say thee, nay!"

Constance pouted, sniffling a little, working

into Alex's guilty conscience. The girl couldn't be that far from home, and taking her there would be the right thing to do. No. She shook her head. Her mind was made, she would not back down.

Impatient with Alex's silence, Constance said, "You will take me, or I shall ... I shall tell my father of your dastardly deeds, deceiver!"

Her eyes widened. Mayhap she had misjudged the girl. "Deceiver? I would never—"

"Protector of women are you? My father will have your—"

"Nay, hush." She sighed heavily. "What wouldst you have of me?" Alex asked softly, covering her eyes with one hand and resisting her strong desire to bolt. She could outrun the girl. It was possible she could escape with her hide intact.

"'Tis plain as day. Take me to my father's house. 'Tis but a short ... distance. I am sure of it."

Guileless, beseeching eyes stared up at her. No doubt she'd ensnared many a hapless fool in her schemes. Alex groaned. Being a hero was no fun a'tall. She really hadn't a heroic bone in her body. All she could think of was getting rid of the girl. She should be on her way. Time was of the essence, and here she sat, bickering like a child.

Lady Constance touched Alex's sleeve hesitantly. "My father will be very grateful to you," she said, a tremulous note to her voice. Her wide, clear eyes filled with unshed tears—a ploy that doubtless had worked on many a man. But Alex

14

was not a man and therefore not given to their weakness.

* * * *

"An it please you, my lady, cease and desist! I cannot keep my mind on our surroundings with your constant prattle."

Night shrouded them in its inky embrace, the light of the moon doing little to illuminate the gloom through the darkened wood. Firedancer jumped at every rustle of leaf, every night insect's song, making her a wreck. Doubtless his nervousness was what had destined him to be her mount instead of some brave knight's.

She looked into the dusky woods, wondering when the days had grown so short. Winter was fast approaching, but Alex felt the heat of hell entwined about her waist.

She knew it was her punishment for her deception—not that she believed she deserved it. Dire circumstances could force even the most steadfast to take drastic measures.

"How testy you are. My father will likely hold great feasts in your honor. Where do you go in such a rush?"

"The McPhersons," Alex replied distractedly. Constance sucked her breath in sharply, unnoticed.

Was that light ahead? Alex raised up in the saddle and peered intently into the dark.

"You can't mean to see them alone? They would roast you alive, pick their teeth with your bones! They are most hideous, odious—"

"Spare me if it pleases you." Constance's

words had finally snared Alex's attention. She knew nothing of her mother's family, and to hear Constance describing her cousins made her throat tighten uncomfortably. Would her only chance for salvation be merely the mists of a dream? "What have they done to earn such a vile reputation in your esteem?"

"'Tis too numbered to count. Just this past fortnight they have stolen much cattle. They have brought terrible humiliation to my father for as long as I can remember. And their women...." Alex felt her shudder against her back. "I'm afraid to even speak of them."

To hear her cousins badly maligned did not bear well with her. Did she truly want to find them and discover firsthand what Constance said was true? What possible reason would Constance have for lying? She could think of none, for the girl displayed no dubiousness of character. She paused, thinking. Unless her cause was to keep Alex at her house—an unwelcome thought she quickly pushed aside.

Were her kin truly thieves? Surely if they were it was because need drove them to it, and she had enough riches they would never go hungry in twenty lifetimes. She felt a sudden onslaught of pity for her relations.

Constance yelped excitedly. "There! 'Tis Derwin Hall! Faster, I must tell my father of all the excitement we have had."

Obliging her reluctantly, she urged Firedancer into a canter—any faster and they risked injury from uneven road and potholes.

The cavernous trees thinned and eventually petered out, spreading open into a wide clearing as far as she could see. No longer obscured by growth, the stars shown a clear path to a bridge leading across a stream, the babbling water rushing past cleared land to a copse of trees. Ahead, illuminated by moonlight, she could see a massive manor house, almost a castle with its fortifications, but it was clearly being modernized due to the recent building boom. They were a wealthy people, evidenced by the glass windows adorning the stone facade, which also told her something important ... they were at peace, for no lord would be so foolish as to build such a house in war ravaged country. But King Henry had been strengthening his borders, adding castles for his defense. The incongruity of this half-castle struck her as folly when war could break out at any time, especially so near the border of Scotland.

Lights glowed in the night, drawing her eyes. Fires. Fires snaked about its base, giving her pause.

"What are all those lights?" Constance asked with wonder.

Men, at least a hundred, milled about the grounds, preparing for something.... Alex wondered at first if the castle had been besieged. Had she been wrong to think there was no war here? She slowed.

As they neared the bridge, a hue and cry went up, followed by another and another. Alex stopped, still running distance from the bridge.

"How long have you been away?" she asked accusingly.

Constance was unnervingly silent behind her. She wanted to throttle the girl. "Well ... I believe 'twas ... perhaps a day ... well, actually the night before and today as well."

Search parties. A hundred men bearing arms and torches. How long had they been searching? And why had this road not been checked?

"I have seen you to your father's house. 'Tis far enow."

"Nay, I would be trampled if I walked now—see the men approach? 'Twill be all well and good, my father shall wish to reward you for my safe return."

Just get off my horse! she thought frantically as men seemed to swarm around them, pushing them forward on the grounds. Someone helped Constance off the horse, and Alex was pulled unceremoniously down. A groomsman took her reins and Alex snatched them back only to have them taken again just as a bellow echoed over the crowd.

Chapter Two

The torch-bearers merged in mass, surrounding them, their faces grim, silent, as though awaiting an execution. Constance chattered joyfully, ignorant of her own folly, or perhaps blatantly ignoring it. Alex heeded not her words, escape foremost in her thoughts.

They'd abducted Firedancer. Without him, she had no hope of reaching her destination, no hope of success. So she waited. She knew not what would become of her, but a dread presentiment crawled into her mind and lay heavy on her breast. She did not wait long.

The hum of Constance's chatter ceased abruptly, and a prickle of unease danced across Alex's spine. Sensing the change overcoming the crowd, she slowly turned, fearing the worst, and found herself faced with a wall of shining armor.

19

Alex became aware of sounds she hadn't heard before: the creak of leather buckles holding plate in place; men talking in awed, hushed tones; her own harsh breathing. She felt as though her mind had been clouded—but it had, and by her own foolishness.

Flames twisted and flickered, reflecting off polished metal and shining into her eyes.

Her eyes focused on the breastplate before her, steel etched by a master hand—whorls and vines twined into a crest held aloft by wolves. Inexplicably, she felt a thrill of excitement. She blinked and looked up, and up, her lower jaw remaining fixed level while the rest of her face turned skyward.

A strong jaw came into view first, covered in faint, dark stubble, clenched in anger. She followed the line as she would with fingers, like a caress, up past his cleft chin to his full, grim set lips. She swept past his nose, broken at least once—a man who likely enjoyed battle. But when she reached his eyes ... she shuddered, her unnerving flights of fancy disappearing in an instant. Dark, perhaps deep sapphire, they pierced her with intense scrutiny, like a lance seeking and finding its target. She was looking into the most fascinating, forbidding face she'd ever clapped eyes on ... and his attention was fixed on her. Half limned in golden flame light, half in shadow, he looked as fierce as a pagan of ancient lore.

A strange, womanly sensation assailed her. It had taken but a moment to take him in fully, but she was disconcerted to find she hadn't had her fill of gazing upon him. She felt warm inside, inexplicably weak and giddy.

She suspected she driveled on herself. Alex shut her mouth with effort and swallowed. She felt a dumbstruck fool—she would surely give herself away, staring at him like a simpleton. In annoyance, Alex waved away moths that had congregated to the torches and their body heat.

"I'll have your head for what you've done," the man ground out, grabbing two massive fistfuls of her doublet. He lifted her from the ground like a bit of fluff, and disconcertingly, she felt her toes dangling. He grunted, though not with the effort. "You weigh naught more than a pageboy."

This was what she'd been taught to admire. Knights in shining armor, protectors of the innocent, men who would conquer heaven and earth for their lady love. She hadn't envisioned herself in the role of villain, however.

Alex was quite taken aback by his implication. Had she done something wrong? Mayhap she shouldn't ought to have stared quite so long. She tried searching her sluggish brain for any other offense, but none came to her. She considered struggling, but it was hardly appropriate for her to start fighting like a she-cat. He'd merely misunderstood.

"Nay!" Constance yelled, a welcome intrusion. Thrusting herself between them, she forced the brute to drop Alex. Alex stumbled back a step, keeping her balance, her gaze never wavering from him.

He looked at Constance in confusion, and Alex

almost smiled. She doubted anyone stood up to the tyrant—ever. Alex wasn't sure why she should need protecting since she hadn't done anything wrong, but she appreciated it regardless. He was a mite larger than she could handle on her own.

The man's hands clenched into fists when he looked back at her. Unease tightened like a noose about her neck.

Saints! He had a foul disposition. If she weren't so certain of herself, she might be frightened. Any other fool would be, but not she.

"You don't know what you've done, Constance." Each word came out slowly, as though he was pained to utter them. "Get you to bed, woman."

"I will not leave while you tear him limb from limb, Bronson. You are my kin, and I love you, but...."

Alex tried to make words come out but her throat had dried of a sudden. She swallowed convulsively, forcing moisture down her throat to loosen her vocal chords. "Mayhap if I introduce myself...." she squeaked.

The man, Bronson she knew now, glared at her whilst another, younger looking giant laughed and spoke up, "Good god, Constance, the boy hasn't even become a man! Listen how his voice breaks."

Alex gaped at him. How dare he? she fumed. She was certainly old enough to be a man ... well ... Certes!

"Oh, Rafael." Constance giggled, confirming

Alex's earlier suspicion she was an airling.

A fluffy moth flew drunkenly around her face and she blew it away. "I will expla—" The world went black in one of her eyes. She yelped in a most unmanly manner, clamped a hand over her eyes, and flailed her free arm in the air in a vain attempt to clear it. "Damn! Remove those blasted torches from my presence!" Tears streamed down her cheek.

"What has happened?" Constance attempted to pull Alex's hand from her face.

Alex wiggled from her grasp as a child would evading its mother. "Leave me be woman. Those foul torches have attracted every insect for a fortnight."

Constance started giggling, uncontrollably, which was bad enough, but then the distinct sound of male laughter began bellowing forth from her cruel inquisitors.

"'Tis not a matter of humor. Doubtless I shall be blinded in this eye and live with the damnable insect in it the remainder of my days."

"Come, let me see it, boy," Bronson said, his voice over gruff and impatient. Mortified, she knew he had laughed also. She attempted to evade him, but he caught her in her susceptible condition.

Bronson grasped her chin, engulfing it in one massive hand, and tilted her face up. "You're as soft as a babe's bottom. No doubt just out of swaddling yourself. Open your eye, lad."

Her arms dropped to her sides in defeat. Was he implying she was weak? "I can't." She

23

squeezed her eyes tightly shut. Alex wouldn't put it past him to poke one of those enormous digits in the offended lid.

"You will."

Something about his tone brooked no argument. Her lids had grown heavy as an oaken chest. She strained to lift them and looked into his face. Someone held a torch near and she flinched, expecting more flying monstrosities, but the grip that held her was firm.

He brushed a callused thumb and forefinger near her eye, holding it open wider, looking closely. His brows were pulled low over his eyes, lending him a grim appearance. Her insides felt quivery again, but she knew it was merely fear of discovery, not those large hands, that made the wash of weakness flow through her veins.

He released her suddenly, rubbing the hand that held her as though he'd been burned. "You'll live. The wound was not mortal." The other armored men began chuckling anew, earning them a glare from Alex.

Her eye did feel better though, and she rubbed it absently.

"I suppose we'll have no killing tonight," the third man spoke with a grin, obviously the youngest of the three.

"Come, Father is awaiting your safe return to his house. We will speak inside." Rafael took Constance's arm and began leading her away.

"I must needs be on my way. If I can have my horse...." Alex whirled around and started running when she was pulled to an abrupt halt, one foot suspended in the air. Craning her head around, she saw it was Bronson's hand fisted around her cape.

"Mine father wouldst speak to you as well, pup." His expression was quite serious. He looked accustomed to having his way in every matter. Well, she would teach him he could not bend her to his will.

As he dragged her across the grounds, Alex had a terrible suspicion she was drawing close to the wolves' den.

Chapter Three

Bronson ushered a reluctant Alex through the great door of the manor, through an immense two story hall, and into the parlor off to the side. They were alone except for Constance and the two other armored men who stood watchfully silent.

Now that they were inside, she could see all three men bore a striking resemblance. Brothers no doubt, and Constance their sister. All shared the same midnight hair, the same dark eyes. Bronson, she decided, was the most handsome, for she was accustomed to men with some age to them, not fresh faced youngsters with no life lived.

The other two possessed an ease about them that Bronson did not share, however. She wondered if they felt uncanny having someone so close to them in appearance, having siblings. She had no experience in such matters.

Turning slowly, she surveyed the room they

were in. Gold plates, encrusted with jewels around the outer edge lined the great mantel, two passant wolves forged into the stone as support. Fine tapestries, depicting the hunt and other histories hung about the walls, woven in a fantastic array of color. Glastonbury chairs flanked the massive hearth, padded with cushions embroidered in scarlet and gold. The two other armored men lounged near the fire, having stripped some of their plate for comfort.

It was a room built for leisure and to impress, and she was not immune to its charms.

The ceiling stretched far above them, and trophies adorned the heights of the walls. Riveted, she stared wide eyed at the vast multitude of antlers lining the wood paneling in orderly rows. The ivory of the horns was a dramatic contrast to the rich, burgundy painted paneling, capturing her attention as effectively as a rabbit in a snare. Her eyes flashed on sconces decorated with bone, to a candle beam crafted completely of horns and lighted with an abundance of precious candles. There were hunters here, and by the look of it, very, very skilled hunters. Alex's collar shrank around her throat.

"Who bested these defenseless beasts?" Alex asked.

"We did, generations of Blackmores," Bronson spoke from behind, coming around her. At her look of horror, he said, "We hunt for food. No animal who dies, dies in vain."

The door flung open and reverberated soundly against the wall, cutting off further questions. A man who could only be the lord of the manor stomped inside with the gale force of a thunderstorm.

Alex cringed, expecting beatings to be handed out, but Constance showed no fear in the face of her father's wrath. Constance beamed at her father. "Papa, you will be so pleased by what has happened."

Her comment was answered with a brain-rattling roar, unintelligible at best but no less fierce for its perplexing denouement. His cheeks flushed dark with ire, began to glow red and darken to purple. "What on God's green earth do you speak of? We have been scouring the countryside for you! We'd just begun preparing to assault those devil McPhersons. You have driven us mad with worry." He pulled her into his arms for a great hug, then released her hesitantly.

"Oh, Papa." With a giggle that seemed to suggest Constance had not heard the threatening sounds that had come from her towering father, she said, "This young gentleman, Lord Alex Montague, rescued me. Lord Montague, this is my father, Lord Derwin." Constance's hand wrapped protectively around Alex's upper arm.

Her words seemed to dawn on him. "Rescued you?" came the ear-shattering reply.

"Now you know better, Papa. We shan't have you going into another apoplexy."

The mention of apoplexy seemed to reign in some of his fury. Lord Derwin looked suitably chagrined and slightly less angry. His circulation began to improve, lightening his dark countenance.

For all his bluster, Alex could see he'd do no harm to Constance. He cared for her—that much was obvious in the way he held her close, in how his hands shook when he'd talked of searching for her. Constance was a fortunate girl to have a loving family.

Something told Alex Constance was accustomed to wrapping her father around her finger.

"I believe you have some explaining to do, young lady," Lord Derwin said, sounding as though commanding great armies would be natural to him.

Constance further irked her father as she leaned over and whispered loudly, "Do not fret so. Papa really is quite gentle."

Alex glanced at the antlers on the wall, not quite believing her.

"Remember when you said to me I should explore my horizons?" She looked innocently at her father who, by this time, had cooled to a slow simmer.

He sputtered, but she continued, "There is so much to see at the fair and when I heard the servants speaking of it, I knew this was just the sort of activity you would approve of." Lord Derwin guffawed. Un-perturbed, she said, "The fair was glorious ... but on the way home some dreadfully smelly man that I had ignored at the fair accosted me and had the gall to demand my purse. I, of course, told the gentleman that I would do no such thing. He became quite cross."

Alex thought cross did not accurately describe the man but wisely kept her own counsel.

"A lady simply cannot abound anywhere these days." Constance tilted her chin up. " O h , Papa. You would be so proud! If it were not for Lord Montague ... well ... I shan't have known what I would have done. He bested that dreadful man with his sword, just like in your stories, Papa. He rode his beautiful steed into the clearing like an avenging angel. I nearly fainted, I was so relieved to see him."

Eyeing Alex appreciatively, noticing her for perhaps the first time, he said, "It seems we are indebted to you ... my son."

Before Alex knew what was happening, he embraced her and pounded her with good fatherly humor on the back with breath-taking force.

"It ... it was nothing, my lord. Any true gentleman would have done the same." For this comment Alex was the lucky recipient of another back-bruising hug. With effort, she caught her breath.

"Oh, my boy. I have not heard of such chivalry since my father's days. It does me good to see a man after my own heart. Chivalry is not dead!" he said with a raised fist, as if challenging the gods to dispute him.

"I knew you would be thrilled." Constance smiled prettily at Alex and her father.

"You must allow me to extend my hospitality to you. I will brook no argument," he said, attempting a stern face, a smile threatening.

Bronson had remained in the background during the exchange, silent, but not forgotten, leastwise not by Alex. She studied him from the corner of her eye. His anger and disgust was a palpable thing. If she were to have any trouble, it would come from him, she knew.

It seemed hours had passed since her arrival at Derwin Hall, but in a short amount of time she had already sealed her fate, caught in a mire so like quicksand it was shocking. Of course, she could turn this to her advantage. Before her adventure, she had learned her cousins' castle was not far from this place. Lord Derwin would undoubtedly know of his neighbors.

The situation was not completely abhorrent— Saints!, what could she be thinking? She was far outnumbered here, her danger of being exposed had increased exponentially. What's more, they were seeming enemies of her family, though she'd give her eye teeth to know why.

No, she could not stay. When the first chance to escape arose, she would take it. Until that time, she could not appear rude, lest she arouse their suspicion.

"If it would please milord, the honor is all mine," she said, a hand placed over her heart as she made a sweeping bow.

Bronson grunted from the corner, the arrogant son of a jackal. Doubtless he would take pleasure in her exposure and certain torture to follow.

"Good my boy. My sons welcome you as well." He gave Bronson a meaningful look.

"W-we have not had formal introduction."

"Damn, I have but forgotten my manners. Sons, I present Lord Alex Montague of ... whence have you come?"

"Evenshire, my lord."

"Of Evenshire. My sons," he gestured with his hand and they came forth as he spoke their name, "The thundercloud in the corner is Lord Bronson Blackmore. My second son Lord Rafael, and youngest son, Lord Gray. I have another son, older than Gray, Lord Nigel, but I fear he enjoys the intrigues of court far too much to visit us often."

He had another son? A veritable army of them, all battle honed and wary.

Alex could scarce believe three such giants had issued forth from one maker, let alone four. She pitied their poor mother. Rafael and Gray looked closer than Bronson. Their smiles and the twinkle in their eyes bespoke deviltry. Aye, she could tell by the look of the Blackmores that they were rogues, the lot of them. There was no doubt in her mind that the last was equally as devastating. Alex was thankful she was not susceptible to charm and flattery, nor a fair face.

She realized she had been rudely silent. "And the lady of the manor?" she asked in a quiet voice.

"She has passed on," Bronson gritted out. His ears were devilishly keen.

"My apologies." 'Twas a trial for her to keep anger from her expression. Alex would be glad to see the last of him. He had taken a dislike to her for some reason she couldn't fathom, and she abhorred having someone angry at her for no good reason.

Lord Derwin dismissed Constance to see about readying Alex a room. "We will see you have every comfort. I will not have it spread about that we treat heroes shabbily in my household. You must rest and refresh yourself." He draped his arm around her shoulder as a friend, as a father.

She felt homesick of a sudden and cursed the foul winds of change for her contemptuous destiny.

She sighed. Alex wondered again at her good sense, but it was too late to back out. She would have to make the best of the situation until opportunity presented itself.

"Come now, I will show you myself to dinner and your room."

As they started to leave, Bronson called out, "We welcome you, Lord Montague. I look forward to your stay."

Lord Derwin chuckled.

She caught Bronson's dark look but said nothing as they exited. She felt his eyes bore into the back of her skull until they'd gone, and she was left to ponder his cryptic statement.

What could he mean?

* * * *

"Well, brother, what did you make of the scamp?" Rafael asked, his legs outstretched, and the remainder of his plate scattered carelessly on the floor along with his brothers'. A servant would be by soon to collect and polish it, and return it to their armory for safekeeping.

"I think him a pissant in need of a good whelping." Bronson yawned, stretching like an immense beast of prey. "I'd blister him for being off from home, but I'd likely break his puny bones with one wallop on his arse."

"Ha! You put on too good a show of nonchalance." Gray sat up in his chair, leaning forward. "You're afraid Constance will enamor herself of him ... or worse, ensnare the boy with her charms. He's a touch pretty I say, but women always find that most appealing."

Bronson's arched brows drew low over his eyes. "Nay. Constance has better sense."

"Aye. What possible harm could come from the runt?" Gray laughed at his dark look. "Ah, I see the thoughts tumbling through your skull, you'll listen to naught I say. Enough of this, will you come with us tonight?"

Rafael was on his feet in an instant. "Aye, we have some fair wenches in dire need of your protection."

Mouth tipped in a crooked grin, Gray said, "They'd welcome your sword with pleasure."

Bronson scowled. "You both know me better than that."

Gray chuckled at his fierce look. "He'll have none of it. He's saving himself for his bride." When Bronson looked ready to pummel him, he ran to Rafael and threw his arm around him as they made to go. "Come, brother, he'll know no pleasures until he rids us of the scamp's presence." They left Bronson brooding by the fire.

He sat in silent contemplation for long moments, studying the dying fire, before Constance came back in to bid him good night.

Bronson grabbed her arm before she could leave.

"Brother?" Her eyes revealed her confusion.

"I wouldst speak with you ere you go. Do you speak the truth? That that child bested a man full grown?"

Constance laughed, her manner gone easy once more. Doubtless she thought his fears for her of no pressing concern. "Of course, Bronson. I am not in the habit of telling untruths to father."

Bronson did not believe so puny a boy could have fought and won against a thief intent on his prize. The lad scarce reached his shoulder and was as slender as a girl. Oh, he didn't doubt Constance had seen as she claimed.

He knew the ways of men, however, and suspected it had been arranged by the boy. Lord Alex Montague was after a far greater prize than a mere purse.

"You will have naught to do with him, Constance. I forbid it."

She looked as though she just realized he still held her and pulled herself free. "I am no longer a child for you to protect from every comer. Father is fond of him—"

"Father is fond of everyone. He would take in every stray if he could. Sometimes I must protect even him from himself."

"You cannot do it all, Bronson. And you go soon to your own house, your own marriage." She suddenly looked serious, no more the care free girl he'd thought she'd remain. "I would have mine before I am too gray."

"I do not need be reminded of my obligations, but I will remind you of your place." He could have kicked himself for the hurt he saw on her face. He always managed to say the wrong thing as far as she was concerned. He had little experience controlling females, and Constance was as headstrong as the rest of the Blackmore brood. 'Twas hard for him to realize she stood before him a woman full grown, not the little girl who'd once crawled on his lap, crying for a mother.

Constance blinked rapidly, clearing her eyes. "I will do as father has taught me, you can be assured."

He noted the defiance evidenced by her stubborn chin and squared shoulders as she left the room without turning back. He no more believed she would obey him than she would father.

Father had allowed her her head far too often. He would not allow some deceptive whelp to bring misfortune to their household, nor to her life.

Besides, she was a Blackmore, and she had obligations to the family name. Just as he did, just as his brothers.

Bronson thought of his own engagement with disgust and cursed the chains of duty and honor. As first born son and heir, his life was not his own, far less even than his siblings.

He breathed a heavy sigh and rubbed his stubbled jaw, distracted.

It was time to put the boy in his place.

Chapter Four

Alex closed the door, sinking against it in relief, her knees weak.

Bidding her strength return, she looked at her
surroundings. To the right, a fire burned in the
hearth, banishing night's chill and dark, while a
bath had been prepared thoughtfully near its
warmth.

The bed looked as though shaped from a single
piece of wood, dwarfing the room with its size,
mattresses stacked up to nearly her waist. Scenes
of wolves hunting, frolicking, living were carved
in relief on the head board.

The Blackmore's propensity for wolves un-
nerved her. She felt too much a lamb readied for
slaughter as it was without reminding her of the
predatory nature of men.

Her clothing had been set atop a massive chest
at the foot, and she hoped no one had questioned

37

her possession of a jar of paste.

A polished metal mirror completed the contents of the room. The room was functional, sparse, and perfect. Privacy was all she required.

Her stomach grumbled, but she ignored it. She had been offered food and drink, but she'd declined—too tense to eat tonight.

A bath was the cure for her anxiety, however. She mustn't let it go to waste.

Throwing off her cape and plumed cap, and almost her wig, she decided against removing it. She would wash her hair when she felt more secure. Peering into the mirror, her reflection was distorted, but she could see the beginnings of a bruise blossoming on her forehead. It would be a wonder if she suffered no lasting effects from Firedancer's antics. Blast his training!

She removed her short wool tunic and slashed doublet, dropping them to the floor. Kicking off her shoes, she progressed into the room. Stopping at the bed, she peeled off the short drawers that concealed her sex and flung them and her thick hose onto the bed before moving to the far wall.

Steam wafted through the room as Alex broke through the veil hovering above the water like a mist and eased into the tub. The heat of the water scorched her, but it was a welcome pain that eased the ache of her body and soul. She dared to relax and closed her eyes, sighing in contentment. She'd been on the road far too long....

A frigid breeze blew across her damp skin, banishing her equanimity. Her lids snapped open, and she sucked a sharp breath in at the horrific sight she beheld.

Constance!

Alex huddled in the water, sinking in until only her head remained above drowning level. She summoned the most forceful tone she could muster under the circumstance, "My lady, you must not be here!" Shock closed her throat to only the weakest of squeaks.

Constance shut the door and walked inside, hips swaying, a smile spread across her impish face. Devil take the girl!

She had cleaned herself and dressed in what she supposed must surely be provocative attire. Her sanguine gown made her skin look exceptionally pale, the bodice trimmed in Spanish lace, cut low and tight to enhance her charms. The hanging sleeves were tied up on the shoulders, revealing wide, embroidered undersleeves.

Alex had an ill feeling in her stomach, and lack of food was not the cause. This could only bode ill for her.

"My father assures me 'tis entirely proper for the lady of the house to assist guests at their bath." She pushed her full sleeves up her forearms and grabbed a washing cloth, proceeding toward Alex with the inevitability of the plague.

"Nay!" Alex shrank back. "It is not done, surely not by a maiden." Escape plans whirled through her head with the speed of a diving falcon. Saints! Why had she not barred the door with some immovable object?

Alex rose in the water just enough to snatch

the cloth from Constance's hand.

Constance chuckled, eyeing Alex. "You have strange ways, my lord."

Alex almost laughed herself. The girl hadn't a clue just how strange....

"Get thee gone, woman. You know not what trouble will arise should you be found here!"

Constance ignored her and took the sodden cloth back, rubbing it with soap. Alex caught hold of it again and they tugged it between them before Alex's strength of will dominated and it landed with a splash between her legs. Constance reached for it immediately, but Alex was quicker. She grabbed her wrist, stopping her.

They were close now ... too close.

Alex was furious. "Does your father entrust you to my care so implicitly, even for so short a time? He does not know me. I could take advantage of you."

"Would you?" Constance looked eager, brazen wench, and leaned forward as if to kiss her.

The door slammed open. Alex's jaw dropped as her gaze flew to it.

Lord Bronson stepped through the doorway.

Death.

Destruction.

TORTURE.

Alex gaped at him, her plight forgotten for a finite moment. Midnight hair, unfashionably long, hung loose around his shoulders, framing his face. Far from looking soft and womanish, he had the look of a dark, avenging angel. And she had the distinct feeling he'd known Constance was with her. He had removed his armor, and she could see he was nearly as broad without it. Alex felt better that he hadn't come prepared for battle, but then, she would hardly put a dent in his hide with a mace, let alone her bare hands.

He strode into the room like an enraged bull. "Get off her," he said, his voice deceptively quiet, revealing none of the animosity apparent on his face.

Get off her! If Alex had been able, she'd have been outraged. As it was, she could think of nothing but a chanting prayer—please don't kill me, please don't kill me.

Constance pulled her arm from Alex's nerveless fingers.

"Out," Bronson bit off the word.

Constance wisely said nothing and stood. He held the door open for her then shut and locked it with a key when she'd gone.

"Nothing happened—" She clamped her mouth shut. Her protestations could sound nothing but damning, even to her own innocent ears.

Alex watched his fluid movement across the room, wary, knowing a storm had been brewing and was about to hit. She wondered that he didn't rend her limb from limb, but the distance provided a flimsy, protective barrier. She couldn't help but be impressed with his grace, even in anger. She'd always thought large men clumsy. She certainly felt rather maladroit herself—but this was not her doing!

"What made you think you could put your hands on my sister?" He met and caught her

41

stare from across the room, his gaze near physical with its intensity.

Had he gone blind? She was the one who'd been molested.

Alex glared at him, which was apparently the wrong thing to do.

Lord Blackmore trod across the room, quick as a viper, and snatched her half out of the tub, looking confused when he felt cloth instead of skin in his hold.

Alex started babbling. "I assure you, I have no designs on your sister. I wish to leave as soon as my horse is rested. On the morrow I go—"

"Why are you yet clothed?" He looked down her chest, over her belly to where her body disappeared into the water.

Alex felt her skin scorch as he raked in her appearance. A strange heat enveloped her, hotter than the water. Insanely, she wondered what he would think if she'd been completely bare. She looked at herself uneasily, thankful her paranoia had at least allowed her to think ahead to some dire possibilities. The linen shirt clung to her body, her sparse curves diminished with padding and binding that she dared not remove—not while she was under the Blackmore's tender care.

Thinking fast, she said, "I was washing my garments, milord."

His mouth quirked and he released her to go sliding back into the tub. "We have washerwomen for that." A dimple revealed itself beguilingly, and she thought for a moment he would lose his fierce edge and smile.

He did not, and he said no more.

Sitting on the tub's edge, he measured her with his gaze.

Alex shifted, uncomfortable with his assessing scrutiny. Her shirt had caught air when she'd landed, and began floating slowly to the surface, baring her with its passage.

Casually as she could, she stealthily moved her hand and pushed it back down.

He seemed not to notice and said, "I know why you are here. At first, I thought you some lord's catamite, for you are far too comely to go unnoticed at court, but I have seen you eyeing your surroundings, judging our numbers, sizing up our holdings."

What the devil was he speaking of? "I assure you—"

"Cease your prattle. I will say my piece and go." He paused a long moment and met her eyes. "You will stay away from my sister. She is spoken for. I will not have some pissant fortune hunter trailing after her. Blackmores do not break their vows."

Without giving her the opportunity for rebuttal, he stood, gave her a last calculating glance, and walked away.

Her drawers lay like a white banner across the deep burgundy bedcovers. They flagged his attention now as he passed. He stopped and seized them from the bed.

"What ... are ... these?" He held them in one hand like a loathsome serpent, a look of horror etched on his handsome face.

43

She gulped. "N-nothing. They are my drawers." They were a design of hers that she'd made for wearing under her tunic, which hung mid-thigh on her rather than upper thigh as most men wore. She'd felt naked without something covering her modesty and wearing a cod piece felt absurd. Since no one would see them, she hadn't seen the harm in making them appealing to her eye.

The answer failed to satisfy him. "There is lace on...." Words failed him. With a visible shudder, he dropped them as though burned and stomped from the room, mumbling something that sounded distinctly like 'damned applesquire.'

Alex sighed in relief when he'd gone, quaking. The worst was over. She'd thought for sure her ruse was finished. She laughed at herself and then at Bronson until tears came out of her eyes. Oblivious man that he was, he'd never suspect a female capable of deceiving him. She collapsed back, weakened for some inexplicable reason.

It was a shame she was not more womanly, that she possessed no feminine charms. It angered her suddenly that he hadn't seen she wasn't a boy. How could he be so blind? She hit the water with a fist, splashing it everywhere, absentmindedly scratching at her wig.

Her scalp itched abominably beneath the loathsome thing, but she daren't remove it. There was no privacy guaranteed a'tall here. She would take no more baths inside the house. 'Twas far too dangerous when all and sundry pranced in and out without a by your leave.

Alex regained her strength and stepped from

the tub, preparing for bed. She'd had enough excitement for one night. In the morning, she'd hie herself off to her cousins. They could not be any worse than the Blackmores, and she had no interest in imposing herself on strangers ... nor her enemies.

Glancing around, cautious, she slipped off her shirt and tried to wring some of the water from her bindings. She groaned. They were still soaked but she would stomach them. She slipped a new shirt on as well as her doublet, tunic, and hose, feeling every bit as though she were strapping on armor.

The heavy clothing was uncomfortable, and she could already feel water seeping through the first layer, but it was preferable to being found without protection. She could hardly contain herself at the thought of dressing as a woman. She was exhausted by her charade and, unreasonably, put out that she'd succeeded at it so well that she was now considered a threat to a young maiden's virtue. Damn their hides!

When she'd set out on her journey, she'd had no idea the difficulties she'd encounter. She was looking forward to becoming the person she was meant to be instead of hiding. Once she was transformed by her cousins, she would come back and taunt the odious Lord Blackmore. He was in sore need of learning a lesson.

Happier than she had been in weeks, Alex blew out her candles and dropped into bed, determined to meet her destiny on the morrow. Her eyes drifted closed just as she heard the alarm raised.

Chapter Five

Alex bolted from her bed in an instant and raced to the window. The grounds below crawled with activity, men scurried about like bees defending their hive from a bear.

What could have happened? Indecision gripped her in agony, her curiosity strangling her sensibility. Should she venture out or stay?

The door slammed open and Lord Blackmore swept inside like a dark cloud.

Alex began to suspect he'd been raised in a barn. "Do you always enter a room thusly?"

He grinned then, and her eyes widened at his transformation from dark warrior to ... to a handsome man. She felt a shiver course over her and cursed her damp garments.

"There are games afoot. Come, I will see this prowess in battle you possess. I see you've already prepared."

Was that admiration gleaming in his eyes?

Reluctant, she accompanied him. He'd successfully dashed any enthusiasm she'd once held. Her choices were rather limited, after all. A young buck would never turn down the chance at ... battle? "Where are we going?" Suspicion tinged her voice.

"The McPhersons are raiding. We are going to stop them."

"So ... 'tis true then? They are thieves?"

Blackmore spared her a backward glance as they descended the stairs. "I thought 'twas obvious."

Doubtless their enemies had compelled them to steal or die. Her enemies—she must keep that clear in her mind. "Then they must surely be driven to thievery."

He laughed, a mirthless bark of sound. Alex suspected he thought her a fool.

"A more odious bunch could not have been created by the dark one himself. Nay, they do not do this out of need. It is spite, pure and simple. You'd do well to remember that."

How dare he talk that way of them. If she'd thought it'd do any good, she'd skewer his arse with her rapier. She shot lancets into his offensive hide.

They reached bottom and threw open the door leading into the courtyard.

Their horses had been prepared, and she could see his two brothers awaiting their arrival. They wore no battle gear, save their swords, and looked eager to be about their business.

They were far too darkly handsome for her comfort. She was accustomed to grayhairs in her grandfather's house, not young, virile warriors too comely for anyone's good.

She noticed all activity on the grounds had ceased and they were alone. Her steps slowed, and she lagged behind. "Will it be four only going?"

He turned to look at her, his face smug. She wanted to hit him.

"Worried?" Blackmore taunted. The jackass.

"Nay. I thought perhaps 'twas your inferior numbers which kept you from apprehending the raiders."

The youngest brother, Gray, recognizable by his leanness, laughed. Doubtless in a few years he would surpass his brothers' monstrous size.

A look from his eldest brother quelled his laughter, somewhat. Rafael frogged him in the arm and he was silent.

"That would defeat the purpose," Bronson said.

"I'm sorry?"

"'Tis none of your concern. This is the way it is done. Now mount up. We ride."

It was her concern. She didn't want to end up spitted for some nonsensical feud of men.

Alex did not see the point of this excursion a'tall. Surely the McPhersons would be long gone by now.

She swung onto Firedancer, who seemed agitated at the excitement. The others took off through the courtyard and Firedancer followed, needing no encouragement.

Casting a surreptitious look around, she could see the Blackmore men smiling. Could they possibly be enjoying this? Was this how men got their jollies?

They crossed into the countryside, over smooth meadows. The full moon cast ample light by which to see, creating the illusion of a cloud covered day instead of the actuality of night.

Lord Bronson led the brood, and she hung towards the back in safety, Lord Gray riding beside her. She wondered if she could slip away in the confusion. 'Twould likely not be an opportune time to introduce herself to her cousins, but mayhap she could follow them to their castle ... Certes! 'Twas ridiculous to believe they'd even be there when they arrived.

Perhaps she could discover their motives by questioning the youngest son.

"Lord Gray?" He didn't answer. "Lord Gray!"

He turned and looked at her. "You need not be so formal. You are a friend of the family now. Call me Gray."

She nodded. "Is this typical for thieves to await their potential captors?"

He grinned, looking wild and very much like Bronson, though his smile seemed not to strike her in quite the same way. "'Tis what they do. They attack, we attack them."

Alex was doubly confused. "You look as though you enjoy this."

"Aye, I do. But don't let that fool you, we all do." He laughed and called to his brother. "Rafael, do we tell him of the time you and

49

Bronson were drug through the pasture?"

Rafael dropped back to more easily speak, his grin wolfish. "Mayhap we should tell Alex when you got hold of one of their she-cats."

Gray growled. "I bear that witch's mark to this day. Heed my words, I'll get the wench for that someday."

"'Twould take a more determined man than you to bring that wildcat to heel."

"And I suppose you'd accept the challenge?"

"Nay brother, I'll enjoy seeing you earn your marks yet again! Mayhap we'll see her once more on this raid."

"I'd welcome the chance." Gray scowled still.

Alex wondered what sort of mark the woman had given such a large man and if their women truly went on raids as Rafael had stated. "Do the women raid as well?" she asked Rafael.

"Aye, if they have the chance, though they dress as barbaric as the men. Gray thought he'd had hold of one of their men, didn't you?" Rafael laughed heartily.

Alex was horrified. If the McPhersons bred women into wild things, how was she to be schooled in the art of being a lady? Her plans began to crumble into dust, and she fell into a morose silence.

'Twas only a matter of time before the king discovered her missing. As a ward of the crown, she would rely solely on his judgment for her marriage. But she had no wish to be a pawn in his intrigues. The only way to avoid it was to be married before discovery, but any man who was caught with her would risk the king's ire, and treason if he chose not to be lenient. She knew that a king's fury at being thwarted would not be an attraction to suitors.

What's more, she had no way of knowing how to get a husband, and she would not make a suitable wife as she was. She had no skills as a woman, since her grandfather had raised her as the son he'd lost to the plague. She wanted only to choose someone safe, of easy temper, a man who would be a comfort to her.

Scotland and her mother's people had seemed ideal, her only hope to escape, but she had been thrust into the midst of this petty feud. Would her kin see her as consorting with the enemy? Oh, what a tangle she was in, to be sure.

"We've arrived." At her downtrodden expression, Rafael said, "Do not look so. You'll see, Alex, their males are far easier to handle." He laughed and rode ahead, Gray scowling in good humor.

'Twas no wonder he was quiet. Dung permeated the air until she could scarce breathe. Why would anyone want to steal such foul smelling creatures? She'd had no idea how much they reeked en masse.

A baritone shout broke the stillness and all hell broke loose.

Wild cries filled the night as the McPhersons and Blackmores clashed. She could see them, their horses circling each other, chasing, chasing, coming to blows when one was caught. How could they think this a jolly good game?

Firedancer, never one to miss action, bucked at his bridle and resisted her frantic efforts to remain safely away from the battle. He ran toward the fray as fast as the wind.

Her nose itched and she wrinkled it, not daring to release her terrific hold on the reins. The tickle persisted, and she realized in horror her mustache was loose. She brought her hand up to clamp over it when a gust of wind blew it betwixt her fingers.

Shrieking like a banshee, with a strength she hadn't known she possessed, she halted and jumped down to the ground, landing squarely in the midst of a dung pile.

In disgust, she looked at her once immaculate shoes. Firedancer sidled, near unbalancing her, then took off into the fray. "Son of a goat!" She shook her fist at the foul beast.

Her lip felt strangely naked without the mustache. Alex sighed. She had spent too much time in this masquerade.

The damned steam from her bath must have weakened the paste. If they hadn't flustered her—no matter. It was done. She must fix it.

Squishing into the meadow, she remained heedless to the roars and clanging of her comrades, her eyes fixated on the dark ground. If she couldn't locate it, they'd know. All of them. Her heart began pounding as her fear increased.

There! She was near tears when she spotted it. Fluttering in a soft breeze, the mustache clung precariously to a pile of dung like the frail petal of a blossom. 'Twas a pure miracle she'd found it.

Alex felt a hysterical laugh bubble from her lips, but she beat it back in submission.

Nose wrinkled, she bent and reached for it with the tips of her fingers just as a jolt from behind hit her, knocked her feet from under her, and immersed her in filth.

A string of curses she hadn't known she knew erupted from her throat. Her fury disappeared when she saw the savage who had unbalanced her. His hair was plastered to his head with something like mud, and hung in thick tangled locks about his shoulders. He was half naked, his face and body painted with strange markings that shone in the moonlight. He looked like some sort of wild creature of the forest, mayhap a brownie. What shocked her most, however, was that he looked at her as though faced with a ghost.

"Heather? Is it you lass? Have you come back to us?"

'Twas her first time hearing the Scots brogue, having never heard her mother speak in her lifetime, and she was surprised at his awful clarity.

She thought her astonishment could not scale greater heights. He moved close, and she scrambled back in the mire on her backside, watching him warily.

How had the devil known her mother's name? Unless....

Her mouth dropped open. She could only be staring at one of her relations. Seeing someone she was related to dowsed her like ice water. A small gasp tore from her.

"Here, lass, before they come." He speech

was rushed as he stretched his hand out for her, his look beseeching. The temptation to risk going was unbearable, but her mind whirled with consequences should she leave now. Would she hinder him? Would he not escape if she went along?

Thundering hooves eating the ground grew loud in her ears.

He looked up, startled. "I'll get ye out of their clutches, lass, don't worry yer pretty head. I'll be back." The strange man looked as though it killed him to leave and ran off, disappearing into the night.

"What on god's green earth are you doing down there?" Bronson yelled at her from behind.

Uh oh.

She remembered her bare lip, the mustache clutched in a death grip in her hand. She slapped it on her face before turning to him. Grimacing at the filth holding it on, she looked at him and searched her mind for some excuse.

"I—I ... was unseated by one of those savages. As you can see, we fought."

"Oh, aye. I can see something has happened." He laughed at her. Laughed. At. Her.

His brothers rode up, and when they clapped eyes on her, began laughing as well—deep, baritone laughter that raised her ire. If they had better sense, they would fear her wrath.

She reached a hand up for help, but one look at her palm and they backed away, laughing so, that they could not even speak. She stood with as much dignity as she could muster, accepting no help from the ogres, which they hadn't offered regardless. "I don't find what is so humorous—"

Their laughter drowned out her words. Louder and harder. She hoped their bellies ached when they were finished.

Bronson held his stomach, and she strongly suspected he wiped tears from the corners of his eyes.

She fumed silently, waiting for their mirth to come to an end, though it showed no signs of abating. Firedancer walked up, her only ally among enemies. She reached for his reins, smiling. He lowered his head to nuzzle her and sniffed, then snorted and tossed his head.

Traitor.

"Oh ho! His own horse will have naught to do with him!" Gray said. As far as she was concerned, she would welcome not hearing another word uttered from his mouth the rest of her stay.

They were men full grown, too old to act in such a way.

"Aye, he looks as though he wrestled a dung pie and lost!" Rafael shouted. "'Twas that which unseated him. Shot up from the ground and attacked."

"They're a dangerous lot!"

"The McPhersons walk on two legs, boy, not hide and wait on the ground. You'll know better next time," Bronson said, curbing his mirth.

Restraining her anger, she grabbed her horse's reins and swung into the saddle. Her toes squished in her shoes. She probably did look as ridiculous as she felt.

"You fail to realize the brilliance of my strategy. We fight battles in a more sophisticated manner in Evenshire. This ... substance catches fire quite easily, why, if my horse hadn't unseated me, you all would have beheld a grand sight."

Bronson smiled, looking years younger. "If that is modern warfare, I want no part of it."

"Oh, you'll see much more than that when I'm done with you. I have ways of fighting you cannot comprehend."

"Nor want to," he replied, grinning.

Alex chuckled evilly despite herself and bowed gracefully from the saddle. "For your insult, you may ride downwind of me." With that, she took off and they chased her, laughing all the way to the manor.

Perhaps they weren't as loathsome as she'd first supposed. Perchance she could come to like them.

They rode into the courtyard and dismounted, their horses led away by sleepy-eyed groomsmen.

Rafael and Gray stripped to their hose and cod pieces and began washing off in barrels of water left out expressly for that purpose.

Snatches of their conversation drifted to her on the wind as they caroused and bathed.

"Ah, Rafael, you should have seen the beauty I had to leave this night. Mayhap she still awaits...."

"How much did you have to drink before you saw her, Gray?"

"No more than usual. I am not foxed. Did I look foxed out there tonight when I had hold of that devil? Besides 'twas a damned inconvenient interruption to my wooing."

"I was under the impression you only wooed in the morning. Mayhap you best. Your vision is much improved with light."

"Oh, aye, mornings are my forte. But takes the night to properly woo a woman, surely you think only of your own experiences—why do you laugh?"

"'Tis nothing. I merely thought you preferred them unconscious, as they surely must be so early in the day."

She found the men entertaining, but the smile fell from her face, and she stopped listening as Bronson neared her. He shrugged out of his doublet and undershirt as he approached her where she stood rooted to the ground. His hose clung to his legs like skin, his cod piece capturing her gaze.

"We wash before we enter the house," Bronson said to her.

"You most of all," Gray shouted behind him.

Their words came to her as though underwater. Her blood rushed in her ears, deafening her. Her eyes were level with his chest now. She'd known men were built differently, but she hadn't imagined there was quite so much difference.

His chest was wide as an oak and looked just as hard and sturdy, muscles and sinew all delineated in perfect precision. Hair encircled his nipples and chest in an intriguing pattern that trailed down his rippled stomach and disappeared into his hose. She wondered where it went, and her eyes strained to follow, her body leaning unconsciously forward.

Alex shook herself from her waking dream and met his eyes. She'd never felt so petite in all the years of her life. A warm, mellow heat suffused her limbs. That strange weakness had returned, swallowing her defenses. Moist heat throbbed between her legs, achy, pleasurable.

Alex looked up, following the movement of his lips, fascinated as they formed words she couldn't decipher. She might have been deaf for all she listened. She wondered what it would feel like to have those lips brush against hers…. She blushed at the direction of her thoughts, struggling to maintain her composure.

His words finally caught her wayward thoughts, thrusting her into the present. Her voice found, she said, "I am afraid I cannot bathe. Not down here." Of its own accord, her gaze kept creeping down to his chest and stomach. And the cod piece! That huge cod piece that locked the beast in its cage. Blasted eyes! She rubbed them in revenge, remembered how filthy she was and stopped. She only hoped she didn't go blind.

Bronson studied her, a strange look on his face, one she'd never seen before and couldn't begin to decipher in her limited experience. "Whyever not?"

"Pox scars. They're hideous. I would spare you."

"You are most kind." His hand shot out and gripped her jaw, tilting her face from side to side. "I see no scars here."

Was his hand lingering? She sincerely hoped not. Never in her life did she anticipate exposure more than now. He was so very large, his hands huge and encompassing and deliciously rough from sword play and God only knew what else.... What was wrong with her that she'd lost her concentration and hoped he'd reveal her for the woman she was?

Not trusting herself to say more, she remained silent. When she said nothing, he released her. "Very well. Go upstairs to your room."

She wasted no time and scampered inside quick as a mouse, away from danger. Away from all that hard, tempting flesh.

Chapter Six

Inside, all was dark and silent. The only sign of her passage—a trailing, redolent cloud of odor. Apparently, Derwin Hall was used to these midnight raids, which she found odd.

Weary beyond belief, she climbed the stairs to her own room. She was not accustomed to the out of doors and did not appreciate her smell. How foolish she was to think him attracted to her. And she certainly didn't want him to be attracted to her as she was—a young lord. She shuddered at the thought.

Alex shut the door, then searched about for additional barriers. Spying the chest at the foot of the bed, she struggled and pushed until it blocked the door.

Satisfied, she eased out of her ruined doublet and noticed her own crude reflection in the mirror.

It was cloudy and warped, but she laughed at the bedraggled picture she presented. She looked as though she'd been dragged through mud by her hair. Only her face remained virtually untouched.

Her wig would need washing she saw. And her hair beneath. The mustache would also—she gasped and leaned closer. It was upside down! She looked at it in horror, as one would a third eye grown on one's forehead.

Had they noticed? She tried to remember and then chuckled at her own foolishness. If they had, she would not be standing here now.

She giggled as her hysteria eased. Thankfully, her clothes had borne the brunt of the grime.

She tried to think of what to do. She couldn't summon a bath, not at this hour, and she couldn't go back downstairs....

Alex paced the room, going to the window and looking out at freedom. An insane thought struck her, one she would never dare had misfortune not pressed its thumb upon her head.

She stripped the bedcovers back and tore off the sheets, gathering more from the chest. She was not but on the second story. The grounds were quiet since the expected attack had come and gone—she'd seen that outside.

She would go to the river and bathe. If no folly befell her tonight, she would make ready and use it as a means of escape the next.

'Twas harder than she'd expected to knot the sheets and tie them together, then tie them to the bed. Her hands ached, but she was satisfied the results would hold. Opening the window, peering down and seeing no one, she threw the make shift rope out, gratified to see it was long enough to reach the ground.

She had a more difficult time going out. Strange how she'd never known she had an aversion to heights until now. Her legs dangled against the wall as she sat on the sill, debating.

Enow! Gritting her teeth, she turned carefully and took the plunge.

The bundle of clothes she'd tied around one shoulder and her neck near strangled her as she went over, but she wouldn't spare a hand to ease her strangulation. She'd trust in god not to pass out before she reached bottom.

The going was slow, painfully so, but her feet touched the blessed ground before she knew it. She regretted having to go back up but shrugged. She would tackle that obstacle when she came to it. Almost tempted to kiss the earth, she bounded off toward the stream, unaware of the shadow that detached itself from the manor and followed her.

* * * *

Bronson was making his last rounds when he noticed the ribbon of white that burst through the lighted window and flailed against the wall like a lonely vine.

He stepped into the shadows without thinking, watching in shock as the boy hung over the edge. His heart dropped to his belly. The damned fool! He'd splatter on the unmerciful ground.

The boy sat in indecision. Bronson had just

recovered enough to find his voice to warn the boy of his folly when he thought better of it. He would see what the scamp was up to first.

The lad had rankled him all night—an enigma he had yet to solve and was determined he would. He watched as the boy slowly clambered down.

He certainly had no fear, an admirable trait, though one that could kill him. Bronson had been known to make grown warriors quake with his coming, and yet the child knew instinctively that Bronson would give him no hurt, despite the fact that he so richly deserved a good throttle. He hadn't quite decided whether or not the boy would be a serious problem to Constance's virtue, but he would keep an eye on him to prevent anything from happening, all the same.

The boy reached bottom, unhurt, and he re-leased a breath he hadn't known he held.

The lad paused, looking around, then grinned and dashed for the river, following it towards the copse of trees that had yet to be felled.

What was he up to?

He followed at a distance now that he'd seen where the boy headed. He kept to shadows when he could, but the land was clear much of the way and he was forced into the open most of the time.

Bronson reached the dark woods, allowing his eyes to adjust to the dimmer surroundings. Splashing sounded ahead and he moved with stealthy quiet through the trees.

A small pool formed in a clearing, moonlight glimmering upon the water like flashing stars. The boy moved into the light, into the water's edge, his hose and tunic gone.

He was merely going to take a bath—had been too shy to bathe with the others. Disgusted, Bronson was about to leave when the lad pulled off his shirt.

What the devil had he wrapped about himself? Thinking the fool had sustained some injury, to the chest no less, he paused in his steadfast approach as the boy unwrapped the bindings and revealed what was beneath.

Bronson stood stock still, blood rushing in his ears, his thoughts running chaotic through his brain. He blinked slowly, staring hard to be certain, not quite believing. The boy was a girl! And not just a girl, but a woman full grown if the rounded shape of her breasts were any indication of age. His head rushed with a mixture of lust and the furious pound of blood.

He watched in astonishment as she pulled what he now knew was a wig from her head and shook out an abundance of crushed curls. An unbidden longing to see their color gripped him.

She bent, lithe as a doe, and dipped her head in the water, rising up and flinging the soaked tresses in the air and against her back. He heard her gasp and laugh, saw her breath misted in the cold night air, her nipples hardened in the chill.

Blood pounded in his groin as he raked his gaze over her body, sleek and muscled, seductive as a siren. He licked his suddenly dry lips, a need to taste and touch near overwhelming him. How long had it been since he'd lain with a woman? Known intimacy of the flesh, or felt a woman's lips upon his own? His coddles tightened, drawing up with need.

He clenched his fists and ignored the near pain he felt, watching her bathe in innocence. Indeed, he had been too many a night without a woman to slake his desire—and he felt the neglect with tormenting severity.

Bronson stifled a groan as she slickened her body with soap and rubbed her hands over her breasts and stomach. His hands itched to do the deed himself, and his shaft pounded with a sudden surge of blood. He rubbed his cock, muffling an anguished moan, trying to ease the pressure, but it did no good.

His breath came harsh and fast. He turned away, unable to bear the sight a moment longer, lest he ruin himself. He'd thought her comely enough for some lord's plaything ... and those drawers—they enflamed him now at the thought of her tight bottom encased in them, sheer to transparency, garnished with lace, innocence....

He felt a thousand kinds of fool. Why had he not realized the boy was a woman? Was he so far gone that he could not see the signs now? 'Twas because he'd been blinded by his own presumptions. Never had he heard of a woman daring such a thing—he paused in his thoughts. That was not so. Gray had encountered one before, bore the ill marks to this day.

Could she be a spy for the McPhersons? Was that why she'd failed to attack them on the raid tonight? Hidden on the ground until he and his brothers had won?

It made a deadly kind of sense. Had their games

with the McPhersons turned treacherous? And if not them, who else would have cause to spy upon them?

Bronson knew of only one way to find out for certain—and that was through the woman. He would watch her now, until he could spring his trap.

A plan formulated, he cast a look back at her. She would be finished soon. The pain betwixt his legs increased once more at the sight of her, and he cursed her for his own body's betrayal.

He slipped back through the woods the way he'd come to prepare.

* * * *

Alex cautiously found her way back to the manor, invigorated by her cleansing and the fact that she'd succeeded in at least one thing tonight.

Her 'rope' still hung undisturbed she saw, and she ran to it, practically skipping with excitement.

Alex grabbed a length and started hauling herself up when a dread voice spoke behind her, "Where do you think you are going?"

Chapter Seven

Alex froze and swallowed her heart. Putting on a calm facade, which in no way mirrored her own turbulent thoughts, she dropped back to the ground and faced him, prepared for her doom. He looked inordinately pleased with himself.

"I am going nowhere, my lord. Do you fear I would run away?" She was proud of how smooth her voice when she spoke, belying none of the anxiety she felt gazing upon him. Discreetly, she dared to glance about for an alternate route of flight should necessity warrant it.

"Now why shouldst I think that? Wherefore do you gallivant about in the night, as though you have the run of the manor?"

"I was not aware I was a prisoner, my lord. Had I but known, I would have remained in my room for my allowance of torture."

He chuckled and stroked his chin, looking deep

in thought. "You have a sharp tongue, boy. I wouldst have the truth from you, however. You are a pup, I was much the same as you at your age. Were you, perchance, seeking a bed-fellow to shine your pretty bauble?"

Alex gasped, outraged. "My lord, your mind runs most foul."

"Aye, 'tis the mind of a man." He looked at her in silent speculation, his eyes revealing none of his odious imaginings. "Are you yet untouched? We shall have to remedy that."

She didn't dare answer him, but her throat had closed of a sudden and she couldn't if she had wanted. He moved close, crowding her, a wolfish smile on his lips as he gazed down at her. She hadn't realized before now the potency of his maleness. It thrilled and scared her all at once. An indefinable flutter of weakness assailed her, making her knees watery. She almost wished things could be different, that she wasn't who she was.

Alex eased her back against the cool stone as if she could melt into it, attempting to gain a measure of distance from him, but he remained unnervingly near. If she tilted her mouth just so, she could kiss him. Somehow, the insane thought persisted, and it was all she could do not to enact her madness. Saints, she'd known the demon spawn but for a few hours, but already he weakened her resolve, distracted her from her purpose. She clenched her jaw, feigning anger. "If you must know, I was training. 'Tis something I do to improve my strength."

"I see." He was close enough she could catch his scent, the smell of his clean skin tantalizing her senses, danger a seduction all its own. Alex swallowed hard, trying to clear her head of his enticing scent. If she'd been a 'woman' in this situation, what would he do, what would be different? The fantasy of being trapped, helpless against the wall as he ravished her played out in her mind. She bit her lip, squeezing her thighs tight, embarrassed at her bold thoughts.

"If 'tis strength you need, we shall put you through your paces in the field on the morrow." He clamped a hand on her arm, squeezing, kneading the muscle. "From the feel of you, I can tell you've sorely lacked in training. You feel as puny as a girl."

As a girl! His arrogance snapped her out of carnal fantasy. Furious, she tried to snatch her arm away, but he held tight. She was so angry she didn't think to question his odd behavior. "I am wiry. Not all men are blessed with bulbous muscles 'neath their shirts."

He cocked a brow. "Have you been measuring me ... as I bathed?"

Alex felt her face flame. "Why wouldst I do that?"

"I know not. Unless, perhaps you have not set your eyes on my sister a'tall, but a lord worthy of your perversions."

"Perversions! W-what—" She gritted her teeth, fuming in silence, sure he was referencing his catamite obsession once again. She feared dressing as a young lord may have been unwise.

She was not so vain to think her femininity out-shone her boyish appearance.

At her lack of response, he said, "Mayhap I have acted hasty in my negative assumptions, missed the pleasures to be found in court. One such as yourself could have something to teach me...."

She looked at him, terror in her eyes. He seriously thought her ... that she would.... Saints, the prospect of fulfilling his fantasies hobbled her mind. Her mouth dropped open, forbidden thoughts assailing her.

"I have no idea what this catamite business is but I—"

He released her arm suddenly as he broke into laughter, a bad habit he had developed quickly at her expense. His shoulders shook with his mirth, his breathing harsh and broken as he guffawed.

"Y-you jest?" When he nodded, she punched him in the arm with all her might.

He stopped laughing. She smiled in triumph, then considered the repercussions as his brows drew down in anger.

"Ow!" Bronson rubbed his arm. "Mayhap there is hope for you yet, pup. Come, I apologize for my farce. Get you to bed. No more training tonight." He looked at her meaningfully, as though he doubted her word. Alex thanked the lord matters had not turned out for the worst.

They went upstairs and he confiscated her rope, his face steadfast and serious despite her protestations of innocence. He left her then, a bemused smile on his face that puzzled her. The man delighted in her torment—it was obvious.

Alex flung herself onto the bed, thankful he had developed a sense of humor instead of being ... of wanting.... She shook her head, swearing to think of it no more. Now if she could only have him wield it in another direction....

Closing her eyes against the fire's dim light, she went to sleep, the soft image of Bronson leaning close for a kiss teasing her mind.

* * * *

Alex was driveling happily into her pillow when her warm blanket was torn from her body.

She drew her legs up to her chest and shivered in the cold air, wondering when her fire had gone out. Mind enshrouded in the fog of sleep, she had only enough fortitude to recover her warm bedcovers. Groaning, eyes closed, she groped for the covers to pull them back on. Fingers straining, searching, she encountered the bane of her existence instead of soft, comforting cloth.

"Get up, boy. 'Tis time for the training I promised you last even'." He sounded decidedly cheerful. 'Twas unnatural. She would rattle his brains for disturbing her slumber.

Alex mumbled something unintelligible, words too much a trial to speak, and buried her head in her down pillow, her arms clutched around it in protection. Her peace lasted but a moment when two massive hands encircled her ankles and pulled.

Alex came up with a godawful shriek, kicking her legs and swinging her arms in retaliation, teeth bared to strike as she growled at her assailant.

The hands released her abruptly, and she slid

to the floor on her arse with a loud thump. She blinked sleep from her eyes and looked at hose covered calves, up past that disturbingly large codpiece and stomach and chest, all the way up to Bronson's crooked grin, his face gray in the half darkness of morning.

She glared at him.

"Wildcat in the morning, are we, Lord Apple-Squire?"

"Be careful lest I show you my claws. And do not call me such names." He chortled and she kicked at his calf, caught it with her toe, and grimaced.

"You foul belswagger. You hurt me!" she yelled and kicked him again.

He sidestepped her this time, a frown hovering on his face. "I hurt you? You have called the kettle black in your idiocy." He rubbed the hurt she caused, chuckling.

"Why have you awakened me at this godforsaken hour? The sun has not yet arisen!" Alex gestured at the window with a limp wrist. He arched a brow, nearly smiling to incur detriment, and held a hand out to her. Alex ignored his proffered hand and stood on her own, legs weak, her fury simmering below the surface. She hated being awakened—at any hour. If she was asleep, it meant she did not want to be awake.

"I informed you why, whelp, now let's be off to break our fast."

Alex planted her hands on her hips, stance unyielding. "Basemecu!" The word escaped her before she'd scarce known it. When his eyes darkened, she realized she had said something she ought not to have. She clamped a hand over her mouth as if it would stop the word from ringing in the air.

"Kiss your arse? You watch your tongue, whelp, lest I show you what such language entails."

She blanched, an image rising unbidden into her mind, one that she was certain he hadn't meant to project. 'Twas best she not provoke him further this morning, leastwise until she'd recovered some of her faculties. "A moment, if you please, my lord. I wish to ready myself."

Bronson looked skeptical, hardly to blame in this instance, and ready to argue but he finally said, "I shall see you below in the dining hall." He left then.

She swore to herself to get the key from him when first she could. This matter of bursting into her room whenever he pleased was not acceptable. She was completely vulnerable abed, and could blurt out the truth of her deception if questioned—she'd been known to speak in her sleep of things that disturbed her.

Alex checked and adjusted her wig and bindings, slipped a leather jerkin on over her shirt, and untwisted her hose. Her shoes were disgusting and she could not wear them as they were, coated in mud and other foulness. She hoped only that no misfortune befell her poor, bare feet.

Satisfied, she went downstairs, her procession quiet, and followed the dull roar of noise to the dining hall. She pushed open the door and entered, then stopped. Heavy trestle tables stretched the length of the room, filled to the brim with men eating and cavorting amongst themselves. Their loud antics would like as soon cause an ache in her head. She was tempted to walk back out again when Bronson spotted her and summoned her forth with a wave of his hand.

There would be no escaping now. The black devil had a keen eye and a wicked temper. Feet dragging, she walked up to the head table.

Alex's place was beside Bronson for some reason, and when she reached him, he immediately noticed her bare feet. His intense eyes scorched her toes. She covered one foot with the other in embarrassment, feeling as though she'd walked out her room naked as a babe. His talent for causing her discomfiture was paramount.

"Have you mislaid your shoes?"

"They are ruined, my lord. I cannot wear them."

He spoke to a passing servant and then pointed to her seat. "Sit, eat." A heaping plate of food was placed before her. She pushed it away weakly and nibbled on honeyed bread, sipping watered wine between bites before finally setting it aside. Her stomach had ever been queasy in the morning.

Bronson, she saw, suffered no such drawbacks, his appetite enormous. He cleaned his plate, looked at her untouched portion, then finished it off as well.

He was quenching his thirst when the servant came back and presented shoes to her. She looked at them, shocked, and turned to Bronson. "I cannot wear these, my lord. They are ... women's shoes."

"Aye, I know it. You have feet too small for wearing men's. These will have to do until your own can be cleaned properly. I shall have some-one see to it tonight."

Reluctant, she slipped them on. They were near enough to her own that she'd not break her neck in them, but she felt devilishly uncomfort-able wearing something so revealing of her own sex. Bronson seemed not to notice, however, so she shrugged it off as circumstance alone.

The men seemed to finish at the same time and they filed out for the courtyard, Bronson follow-ing in their wake.

By the time Alex reached out of doors, weak sunlight crept across the sky like dishwater run-ning over muddy earth.

"Good morrow to you, young lord." Gray sauntered up to her, looking as irritatingly re-freshed as his brother. She wished she'd rested as well. Sleeping in a strange house, under watch-ful eyes did not agree with her. And she'd had the most disturbing dreams, dreams of soft, ro-mantic kisses and roaming hands.... She shook her head, irritated at her illicit imagination.

"Good morrow, Gray. Where has your brother gone?" She'd lost him somehow. She couldn't see past the throng of assembling men. Alex was not short by any means, but the men of Derwin Hall seemed bound and determined to dwarf her. She could well believe they only thought her a child.

75

"He is training the men this morning. Rafael has gone, so he cannot see to them for him. I know it does not look it, but we keep a full garrison of trained men here ... for any eventuality. But enough of that. I'm to see to you until Bronson can come, though 'tis like to be half the day before he returns."

Alex soon learned, for all his ease of manner and jests, Gray was a hardened warrior who allowed no weakness in his students, no mistakes.

Grandfather had trained her in the use of her sword because 'such knowledge can always be put to use,' but he had never been so merciless. Gray had no reason to be easy on her, and she felt it in the fiber of her being.

By midmorning, her arms and legs ached abominably, heavy as a broad sword, her feet like anvils, but she'd impressed the unimpressable.

"You've been taught well, young Alex." He wiped his forehead with the back of his hand. "Now 'tis time you learn moves you'll need in battle, when savagery and schooling merge. Are you up for it, lad? Think you can best me?"

"Aye, I know I can." Without another word, she thrust her blade at him and he parried. They circled one another, swords darting in but making no direct hit as the blades clashed and metal screamed against metal.

Alex was determined to prove her worth. The irony of a puny female beating a monster of a man tickled her. She only wished she could take Bronson in such a manner ... or that he'd at least witness her victory.

Abruptly, Gray changed his strategy, and she knew this was what he'd referred to earlier. Gray used fists and hilt, even his legs to battle her, and she felt herself surrounded by him. Nimbler than he, she evaded him, but she was wearing down quickly.

Dimly, she sensed Bronson called out behind her, but she paid him no heed, her mind concentrated on winning. Seeing her opening, she ran at him but misjudged her opponent's own distracted state.

An arm came across her vision, and before she knew what had happened, she was lying on the ground, Gray looking concerned above her. An instant later, he disappeared as a huge, black shape crashed into him.

Her thudding heart eased into its normal rhythm. Catching her breath, she struggled to a seated position. Bronson had hold of Gray ... or perhaps 'twas the other way around. They looked to be trying to kill one another.

"I told you be easy on the boy today," Bronson gritted out, his breath knocked from him as Gray hit his stomach.

"I was," Gray growled.

"You damn near knocked his head off, I hardly call that 'going easy'."

Alex got up on shaky legs, rubbing her soar backside. "What goes on here?"

They stopped abruptly, faces blank with shock, Gray half kneeling and Bronson's beefy arms wrapped around him.

The two men looked so absurd, their expressions so confused, that she couldn't help herself. She started laughing. She held her belly and fell back onto the ground, laughing harder. "Y-you look ... as though ... you are going ... to hug him to death."

Bronson and Gray came and towered over her, faces half grim, half amused. She peered up at them with tear blurred eyes.

"I thought he'd killed you, scamp. I see now nothing could pierce that thick head of yours."

She grinned just as a cry echoed through the air. They all looked to its source. Constance ran to them, her skirts flying out in the wind, her eyes only for Alex.

"My lord! Are you injured?" Constance helped Alex to her feet, worry wrinkling her brow as she fretted over Alex. "Bronson, Gray, you shall be sorry if I find this has happened ever again."

"I shall live, dear lady, fear not."

Alex feigned more weakness than she felt, and Constance glared at her brothers. 'Twas hard for Alex to keep straight as she saw how shame-faced they were.

'Twas how sympathy should be doled out for her, after all. She allowed Constance to lead her away, clucking over her hurts, leaving two be-mused men behind.

She was thankful the girl had come, thankful to escape their rigors. As they walked away, Alex couldn't help but waggle her brows in mischief at the men, and their guffaws tickled her well into the trial she would endure at Constance's tender mercies.

Hours dragged into a lifetime for Alex. She had been deemed too injured to accompany the household for the evening meal and been fed like an invalid by Constance herself.

Eventually, Constance left her, but her respite was brief, for a summons delivered by a pale faced servant came from Lord Bronson to see him in his room.

Alex leaned her back against her propped up pillows, debating on whether to venture forth or not. Doubtless he desired to speak to her of her absence this evening. A longing to taunt him with Constance's attentions brought a smile to her face. Let him think the worst. She would soon be leaving.

Alex swung her legs over the bed and attempted to stand, falling back almost instantaneously as fire erupted in her muscles. She groaned, wishing an early demise would come to end her torture.

Breathing deeply, using her arms for added leverage, she managed to propel herself to her feet. She caught a bedpost and steadied herself with a weak arm. Gray and Bronson would pay for their 'training,' she vowed. Somehow, someday.

Determined, she left her room and was surprised to see the servant awaiting her, and realized she had no idea where Bronson lay his dreadful head at night.

"I am to see you to his chambers, my lord." The pale man bowed and began leading the way.

Alex's stomach began knotting as she neared,

wondering if she was wise to do this in her weakened state. Her body's strength and ease of movement improved with each step, and she tossed her worries aside, eager for vengeance.

The servant left her standing before Lord Bronson's door, hurriedly walking away.

Steadying herself, she knocked three times.

"Enter." His deep voice was muffled through the thick oak door.

Boldly, she walked inside, the door's weight causing it to slam behind her unheeded. Her jaw dropped at the sight she beheld, her eyes large as golden tureens.

She backed up until she was trapped against the door, holding it barred with her body, unable to turn around and leave, her feet heavy as though embedded in stone.

He was naked.

But even his nakedness did not shock her as much as what he said once she'd entered the room fully.

"Take off your clothes."

Chapter Eight

"Argyle, are you certain she's kin?" Hugh McPherson asked, pushing his empty plate aside as a serving girl came to take it.

"Aye, brother. She had the bonny look of Heather, I swear it. 'Twas difficult to see, but I warrant she's her daughter."

Kiara slammed her fist on the table and stood, garnering everyone's attention. Eight pairs of eyes settled their gazes upon her. "Those damned Blackmores are holding her hostage. Are we going to do something about it?" She pressed her palms flat on the table, looking at each in turn with as stern a look as she could muster.

The room erupted into discussion as everyone started talking at once. Hugh, the eldest and patriarch of the family, silenced them by raising his hand. He stroked the braids of his beard in contemplation—a stalling habit that annoyed much of the clan. "We'll need to see if the lass is endangered as you fear first, Kiara. I'll send one of the lads to check."

Kiara laughed. Used to her odd ways, no one took objection to her outburst. "He'll never get past those brutes and you know it."

Hugh's eyes twinkled. "What do you propose, gel?"

Kiara grinned. "That we go inside. I can slip past their guards easily. The Blackmores are so full of themselves, they'd never suspect a wee lass like meself sneakin' in."

The table erupted in laughter.

Uncle Argyle finally caught his breath, stolen by laughter. "God above help them should they catch you, gel," he shouted, grinning and waggling his eyebrows.

Kiara returned his smile. They'd tried before and not succeeded. "'Twill take better than they to lay hands on me."

"'Tis a good plan, daughter. You take Wren and let us know what you see. If you can get the lass out without trouble, bring her along."

Kiara frowned, looking at her older brother. He waggled his fingers at her, grinning, looking entirely too smug for his own good. "I can do it meself," she said.

"You'll take Wren." His tone brooked no argument. "I like not you being at that brood's mercy without some protection."

"And you think Wren would protect me?"

His bushy brows drew down as he frowned at her.

She sighed, wise enough to know when she'd lost. "Very well. But 'tis my plan ... and he must follow it to the letter!" She brightened, thinking of what they'd do to get inside. It might not be so bad taking him along after all....

* * * *

The lock clicked behind her. Alex turned frantically and tried to open the door, to no avail. Realizing her frenzied efforts were useless, she dropped her arms and turned to face Bronson, a morbid tension entering her bones. She cleared her throat and asked, "Pardon me?" 'Twas a noble effort, indeed, to be so calm in the face of his ... his....

He was in the midst of rubbing a soapy cloth on his chest. On his very wide, very hard, very muscular chest. Alex stared, mesmerized as bubbles formed and broke on his bronze skin with each pass of the cloth. The wet sheen glistened gold in the candlelight. She half wondered if he felt as molten and smooth as her eyes led her to believe. A queer curiosity kindled inside her.

Bronson didn't look up from his task, continued running the cloth over his flesh, dipping down his belly, forcing her eyes to follow the line of his movement. She'd leaned forward without realizing it, straightened up when his voice broke through the fog clouding her wits. Saints! She acted like some simpleton.

"I need some help washing my back. If you keep your doublet and shirt on, you shall get soaked." He looked up, arching a brow. "Come, boy, you've seen manflesh before."

Alex blanched. Never in her life had she seen manflesh like this. Somehow, seeing him before in only hose couldn't compare with this. She knew he was completely bare, and the knowledge struck her with intense awareness of how little stood between them. "This hardly seems proper, my lord—"

"Bronson. There's naught improper about it. Mayhap if you were a lady, but we both know that not to be true."

Did his eyes gleam? The corners of his mouth hitch infinitesimally higher? No. It wasn't possible. Alex swallowed, her throat dry as scrub brush in the summer. "Why have you locked me in here?" she squeaked, refusing to let go of the door handle. She thought perhaps if she let go, she would melt onto the floor.

He smirked. "Just a precaution. I don't want someone to walk in and gather the wrong impression. Someone will be in later to bring bath linens. If you hurry, you can leave then."

She narrowed her eyes, scrutinizing him, but he gave her as innocent and blank a look as she'd ever seen. If he'd discovered her secret, she had no doubt he'd have thrown her out on her arse ... or whipped her ... possibly gaoled ... any number of unpleasantness came to mind. No, it appeared he'd decided to take her under his wing as some sort of companion or friend. Men were odd creatures, to be sure.

Frowning, Alex shrugged out of her doublet and laid it atop his mattress. The shirt still afforded some protection, thick as the linen was.

84

She rolled her wide, embroidered cuffs up just above her elbows. If she was to do this, she wanted to be done with it as soon as possible and out of the realm of temptation. Just thinking about the fact he was naked in her presence caused her skin to itch and sweat and her face and bottom to heat as though she sat upon a flame. He was like some dread affliction, and she couldn't think straight looking on him. He'd addled her brains with a fever of the flesh.

"You'll get wet." He wagged a finger at her, grinning.

"I shall survive," she said morosely, dragging around behind him. Never in her life had she seen a man so willing to bathe ... and often, apparently. Trust God's luck to thrust her in this treacherous nest of cleanly brutes.

Alex settled on her knees behind him on a folded length of linen toweling to protect her knees from the hard floor. He handed her the cloth over his shoulder and leaned forward, presenting his back. His shoulders flexed as he circled his arms around his knees. Alex swallowed, rubbing the soap on the cloth in a daze. Up close, he appeared more monstrous than before.

Tentatively, she touched the cloth to his shoulder. His skin twitched with the contact, muscles tense as she smoothed it across the taut line of his shoulders. He relaxed as she scrubbed him, and she found she enjoyed touching him, running her fingers over his hard muscles. The blades of his shoulders indented sharply, and her fingers crept into the hollows as she rubbed, feeling how strong his back, how hard. It was a warrior's back, with a warrior's strength and old wounds. A thin, white scar skated his right flank. Another patch of pale skin roughed his shoulder, as though he'd struck something with it long ago. There were other tiny nicks spread over him—testament to an active life.

Alex tried to imagine how he could have accumulated the scars during his life as she continued washing him ... washing him. She felt an odd warmth, a lethargy, spread through her limbs at the domesticity of the action. A wife would do this for her husband—tend his wounds, ease his tension. Though she could tell he was a wary sort of man. Even in stillness he seemed to move. She was utterly fascinated.

"There is more to my back than the one spot, boy." There was laughter in his rough voice. His shoulders trembled as though he shook with silent mirth.

She blinked rapidly, looking at the red swath of skin along his left side. Getting a hold of herself, she scrubbed his skin mercilessly, eager to be done with the task. What madness had seized her? He tensed but said not a word as she stripped the hide from his bones.

"Lower," he said, leaning forward more.

Alex obliged, moving down his back without thinking, then froze. A sweat broke out on her upper lip. She could see the curve of his buttocks through the water. Dare she? Being in this guise freed her. She'd never dare this as a maiden, but as a man, it mattered not. More curious than she should be, she slipped beneath the water's edge and stroked his buttocks.

They were as tight and round as she'd thought. A well of heat flooded her thighs as she rubbed him. She found herself smiling in pleasure.

"That is enough of that, scamp," Bronson said, shifting in the water, his gruff, husky voice jerking her back to reality. He leaned back, forcing her arms to slip around him so that she could bathe his chest and arms.

Alex's heart fluttered as his damp shoulders touched her breasts. His heat seemed to seep through the linen straight to her flesh. She prayed to the lord that he could not feel their shape beneath the binding.

"Why is it you travel alone, Alex?" he asked as she slid her soapy hands over his chest. His small, flat nipples hardened beneath her palms as they skimmed over him.

Alex's mouth went dry at the sensation of his response. She knew it was not sexual, and yet, she could not help but to fantasize what he would do if she was a woman bathing him. She slipped across them again, smiling to herself.

He cleared his throat, shifting in her arms. "Alex?" he prodded.

She blinked the fog of desire from her mind, realizing he'd asked her something and she couldn't remember what. "Hmmm?"

He turned his head to look at her from the corner of his eye. "Are you avoiding the question on purpose? Wherefore do you travel?"

It was just the sort of questioning she'd hoped

to avoid until she managed to free herself. Alex chewed her lip, grasping his head and forcing him to face away from her as she washed his hair. She searched her mind for a lie capable of convincing him she told the truth. Finally, she settled on a half truth. "I thought to have a tour of the realm before I am married."

He stiffened, tried to turn his head to look on her, but she held him fast. "You are betrothed?" he asked tersely. "Surely not at your age. You cannot be much more than a child."

He almost sounded as though the knowledge bothered him. She wished she'd have thought of another tale to tell him. "I have reached my majority."

He grunted, letting her know he did not believe her. He was silent as she finished his hair, but when she moved to pull away to leave, he stopped her. "You did not finish my chest."

"I thought mayhap your own cleansing was enow."

"Nay, there is more dirt to be washed away."

Alex swallowed as he leaned back once more. She felt entirely too warm at his nearness, to eager to feel the sculpted ridges of his muscles. Her fingertips tingled to touch him. Her heartbeat quickened, and the bud betwixt her legs answered its call, throbbing with awareness. Saints, she was molesting him with her mind and hands, and he, in innocence, trusted her to bathe him. Surely she should be flogged for the sinful turn of her thoughts, but she could not help their unbidden arousal.

She traveled lower, down his rippled belly, fascinated by the difference of his body from hers. He sucked in a sharp breath, his belly jerking as her hand dipped beneath the water, following the thin trail of hair.

"Mmmm," he groaned suddenly, startling her.

If he'd struck her he couldn't have surprised her more. Alex was horrified at the unconscious movement of her hands, at the manflesh she'd sought to take hold. Alex jumped up from the floor, dropping the cloth with a splash. She scooted around him, edging toward the door, keeping her eyes on him lest he make some sudden move for her.

He gave her a quizzical look, one brow arched. "What is the matter?" He raked his gaze down her body. Heat followed the trail of his eyes. "You've gotten wet, Alex. Care for a change of shirt? I have plenty to lend."

Alex glanced down at herself, saw she was soaked through. She hadn't even realized.... Alex looked up as though stricken. "No, my lor—Bronson. I—"

Was that ... something ... bobbing in the water betwixt his legs? Alex gulped, caught between horror and curiosity.

"You can't walk about in that wet shirt. Hold a moment, I will get one for you." He started to rise.

"No, no, no," Alex shrieked. The door opened suddenly behind her—salvation. She pried her eyes off the sea serpent rising to eat her, scooped up her doublet, and dashed for the door, bolting past the maid bearing linens without pause. She fairly dashed back to her room, where she could have at least the illusion—if not the truth—of safety.

Alex slammed the door and leaned her back on it, inexplicably weak.

Dear god above, she'd nearly ruined herself in there! She never ever wanted to see manflesh in her life ever again.

His soap scented her skin, surrounding her in the memory of stroking his naked flesh, in having him pressed intimately against her. He had to suspect her a queer creature, for she knew she acted too odd for her actions to go unnoticed.

Alex sank to the floor, pressing her hands against her hands low on her belly. Her womb ached, clenched on a spasm of pain. She could still feel the race of her blood, and wondered if her reaction to him would only increase the longer she remained in this household. She did not trust herself around him. He was far too comely for her ease of mind. No matter that he thought her only a manchild, he was her family's enemy. She couldn't allow herself to grow soft to him.

* * * *

Bronson paid no heed to the maid who came in and scurried out again almost as quickly. His thoughts centered wholly on the tempting minx who'd escaped him at the first arisen opportunity. He hit the water with his fist, cursing his recklessness and the single-minded beast between his legs.

He'd been so intent on feeling her hands on

him, he'd hardly managed to glean any information from her. What's more, he endangered his mission by allowing her to know she affected him. Her woman's touch had enflamed his blood, however, and he'd been hard pressed to think of anything besides pulling her into the tub and onto his throbbing cock.

His coddles burned with pent-up need, drawing tight against his flesh. His shaft pulsed with desire. He could not fathom why he wanted the woman so badly, but surmised he'd been far too long without a woman or he would not want this strange creature so badly. The girl was resilient, a survivor, it seemed—a trait he found wholly remarkable. He could admit that he admired her determination, even if it was at odds with what he himself wanted.

Bronson knew she would attempt escape rather than face possible exposure. He just had to be sure to keep close watch on her so she would not be able to do so.

The situation was a tricky one, to be sure. He felt unaccountably awkward near her, as if she fogged his mind from reason. He would do well to reign in his lust, mayhap slake his thirst on a willing maid. Bronson scowled at that thought. He was not so weak willed that he could not control himself. And, he reassured himself, he had no plans to reveal her for what she was, not until he found out the true reason behind her guise.

The thought gave him pause. Had she told the truth to him for her travels? Was she attempting to escape her betrothed, or was she, in fact, already married and unwilling to admit it so? There could be way of finding the truth except by tripping her on her own lies. That she lied, he was certain, but when she'd spoken of marriage, it sounded an honest answer … and made a disturbing kind of sense. Many a woman dreaded the marriage bed, not discounting the arrangement. As his father's eldest son, even his own marriage had been arranged.

The thought of some brute or old man plowing into her woman's sheath made his blood boil. Madness overtook him, bade him to find the truth of the matter. If she was a maiden still, she could not be married, but there was a very real possibility that a man claimed her hand for marriage.

He would have no way of finding out if she was a maiden unless he revealed his knowledge of her true identity, and he could not take that risk. His groin clenched with the notion of plunging into her depths, with sinking his fingers into her core.

Bronson rubbed his groin, trying to ease the unbearable pressure, but touching himself with images of her in his head only increased the pain and his sense of guilt of betraying his own betrothed. He had not even seen the woman he was to marry, let alone spoken vows, and already he was tempted to break the marriage contract. For what? For a temptress and a liar who'd more likely steal his family blind as not.

Bronson stood from the water, stepping out onto the toweling she'd knelt on and grasping one of the linens the maid left. His manroot stood straight from his belly, angry and turgid as he rubbed himself dry. He would get no sleep this night.

* * * *

"I canna believe yer forcing me to wear this, Kiara." Wren grimaced at the old dress she'd forced on him.

Kiara giggled, smirking at his expression and stoop. She was a wicked girl indeed, but having the hall laugh at his disguise was worth some punishment in the afterlife. She couldn't help but enjoy teasing him mercilessly. It was the McPherson way.

The servant's entrance door opened briefly as a spry maid stepped out and rushed past them. "Shh," she whispered, huddling close to Wren, turning her face away inconspicuously. "Yer brogue'll surely give us away. And remember, yer an elder woman, so keep yer nose out of the maid's skirts. I canna say I'd miss ye much if they caught ye."

Wren glanced up at the glass facade above them. "'Twill take hours to search."

Kiara nodded. "That is why we're splitting up. I'll check upstairs, and you down. We meet back here in an hour to compare our findings if we have any."

Wren nodded. "Good hunting," he whispered as they moved inside. They said nothing as they passed through the entrance.

Kiara held her breath, awaiting discovery from the servants, but no hue and cry went up, accusing them as impostors. Kiara soon found the servant's stairs and parted ways with Wren, stifling a chuckle as he crept about like an old hag.

She'd just stepped out of the servant's passage into what looked to be a main hall when a familiar male voice boomed through the passage. Kiara froze instantly, her heart thundering in her chest. She flattened against the wall, darting a glance to the source of the voice.

Him!

Another of the Blackmore brutes trotted down the hall toward him. "Gray!" he shouted. Her nemesis stopped, grinning as his brother caught up to him. They spoke in low tones, laughing, boastful sways to their bodies as they continued down the hall.

A murky name for a scoundrel and blackguard if ever she'd heard one. Gray like mud and stone, old manure and foul skies—

He stopped suddenly, and her breath caught as he looked away from his brother ... straight at her. She couldn't hear what he said, but he frowned, and her stomach clenched as his brows drew together.

Did he recognize her? God's teeth, she must look an impostor doing nothing but standing there gaping at him.

Never run from a wolf when it challenges you. They sense your fear and go in for the kill. She had to remember these Blackmores were more akin to beasts than men. With a calmness she didn't feel, Kiara slowly stood away from the wall and began walking in the opposite direction. Her neck crawled with the feel of his eyes on her. It took every ounce of her will to keep from running in panic.

Finally, she reached a juncture and turned, glancing out of the corner of her eye down the hall. He was gone.

Kiara started breathing again. Damn man. How dare he make her feel hunted and ... and scared?

"You there! Come here."

Kiara glanced up from her feet, startled. A frazzled, doughy woman beckoned her forward, her arms loaded with linen. Kiara approached, surprised when she thrust the load into her chest.

Kiara grabbed it automatically, giving the woman a quizzical stare.

She blew her hair out of her eyes. "Take this to Lord Bronson's chambers. He's expecting you. Here's the key. You bring that back down to me when you're done. I have to get back to laundry."

Kiara freed a finger and took the key. "Where is it?" She needed to dump this off and start her search if she was ever going to find the girl.

"New here? Lord, I cannot keep up with the staff. At the end of this hall." She left her then, disappearing back into a servant's door.

Kiara hefted the load, getting comfortable with it, then walked down the hall. She reached the door, listening to muffled voices inside. Not seeing anywhere to set the linens, she struggled with the key and finally managed to unlock the door, wondering why in the world it was locked in the first place.

These Blackmores were stranger than she'd thought.

Kiara opened the door, nearly dropping the linens at the sight of the huge, naked brood leader bathing ... and then the boy in the room turned around with a startled gasp.

God's teeth! She froze, watching in stunned fascination as he dashed past her, nearly knocking her to the ground in his haste.

"Bring those to me."

Kiara nodded, trying to appear meek as she left the linens, leaving as quickly as possible. The boy was long gone, no trace hinting to where he might have gone. But she knew quite suddenly that that had not been a boy. She could practically pass for Kiara's sister.

Something nefarious was going on. That she'd been dressed as a boy and been bathing the head of the Blackmore sons could only bode ill. The door had been locked. The girl was a prisoner, and that Blackmore beast was enacting perversions on the poor girl. Why else would he have her inside, bathing him, if not to seduce her?

And that meant the McPhersons would need to rescue her, for she was certain this girl was kin ... as certain of it as she was her own bloodroots.

Knowing she could do nothing about it so outnumbered, Kiara went back the way she'd come. It would take some planning, of course, but she had a key. If the girl was locked up with Bronson regularly, she could be rescued easily.

She was smiling by the time Wren met her in the courtyard.

"Still gloating over me? How fared your hunting?" Wren straightened slightly, his back popping with the movement. He pressed his hands to his lower back, grimacing.

"Walk with me. 'Tis time we were gone," she whispered, linking her arm with his as though she supported him. Other servants left to go to their homes, and they slipped easily among them.

"I found her," she finally whispered, secure in their safety. He tensed beside her but continued walking.

"And?"

"She is kin, I know it. But that Bronson Blackmore holds her captive. I fear for what will befall her if we don't do something to get her out. I think he means to seduce her, though whether as a boy or girl, I canna tell."

Wren nodded, looking disgusted. "A nest of wolves, to be sure. Their girlchild had hold of me for a quarter of an hour. I thought like as not I'd die from her going on about me being too sickly to work." He chuckled, rubbing his chin. "A pretty, wee thing she be."

"Get yer mind from betwixt yer legs," Kiara scowled, glancing up. Seeing they had passed out of sight of the house, she said, "Come, I tire of these guises. I cannot wait to tell Father my plan was a success."

"Aye, rub it in," he grumbled, keeping up. When Kiara got an idea in her head ... there was naught anyone could do to stop her....

Chapter Nine

Over a week went by while Alex waited impatiently for an opportunity to go to the stables, rescue her horse, and escape. In that time, she'd had an eerie sense that she was being pursued, but surrounded by the brood as she was, there was little doubt why she felt that way. Bronson, she'd decided, was a thorn in her side, best removed as soon as possible lest illness set in.

Finally, when she'd nearly given up hope of disentangling herself from their midst, the Blackmore watch lessened enough so that she had a spare moment to herself. Relieved more than she could ever say, Alex made ready to escape. She didn't gather up her clothing, since that would appear too suspicious, so she went empty handed down the stairs.

Alex slipped out the door, hugging the wall as she peered around the corner to the clearing that circled the manor. In the distance, she could see the men training. To her left sat the stables, free of activity at this time of day. She should know. She'd watched from every vantage point above it enough in the past week to know that after the noonday meal, the stables were left untouched while the men continued their training.

Slowly, Alex straightened and stepped out, cringing in anticipation of discovery as she crossed the harrowing distance to the stable. Reaching the building without detection, Alex pushed the door open a wide crack and moved inside. There appeared to be no one inside. Alex breathed a sigh of relief.

Sunlight streamed through thin spots on the thatched roof and through rough hewn slats, giving the wide, open area a hazy look of summer dusk. On one end of the stables there stood another door, but from the hay coating that end of the building, she surmised it hadn't been opened in quite a while. She would have to exit the front entrance. Firedancer should be able to outrun the men if they traveled by foot, and she'd certainly have a good head start regardless of whether or not they saddled horses and gave chase.

Firedancer, sensing her nearness, poked his head over a gate and whinnied at her. Alex smiled and went to him, petting his nose as he nuzzled one hand. "Did you actually miss me, you ornery beast? I missed you too."

Alex continued petting him, casting about for her saddle when a dread voice interrupted her sparse search and sent chills up her spine.

"There you are. I've been looking for you."

Alex whirled, a smile pasted on her lips. "Lady Constance!" Alex eyed her surroundings frantically, wondering if they were truly as alone as she feared. To her dismay, she discovered they were.

Constance danced over to her, giving her a saucy smile. "Were you about to go for a ride?"

"Uh, no," Alex said. "I just came out to check on this lazy beast to make certain he faired well in your father's stables."

Constance stepped up to Firedancer and began to stroke his forelock. Alex took a step back to put a more comfortable distance between them, tripped over a pail, and abruptly sat. Constance was upon her before she could scramble to her feet. "Oh you poor dear! Have you hurt yourself?"

Alex stood and grabbed her forearms, thwarting Constance's attempt at a cuddle. "Why no, Lady Constance. No more than my pride."

Undeterred by Alex's attempts to hold her at bay, Constance puckered her lips and dove for the kill like a hawk with its prey in sight. Before Alex could gather enough presence of mind to dodge, Constance pressed her lips firmly to her own. If that wasn't bad enough, the hussy stuck her tongue out and licked her.

Saints above! Her first kiss—and it was a girl!

Shuddering, Alex gave her a shove. Unfortunately, she had been too preoccupied to realize that Constance had her in a firm grip as well. As Constance fell backward, she dragged Alex with her, insinuating one leg around one of Alex's thighs. Almost frantic now, Alex fought to break free. The girl was surprisingly strong, however.

The effort quickly evolved into a full scale tussle. When Alex tried to roll away, Constance rolled with her, taking first position on top.

Arching her back, Alex managed to throw Constance off, but the girl's grip was unbelievable. Even as she rolled onto her back, she dragged Alex on top of her once more. Rearing back, Alex placed one hand in the middle of each breast and pushed for all she was worth. It was at that precise moment that Bronson strode into the stables and came to an abrupt halt, his face darkening like thunder.

"What the hell?"

The bellowed words were enough to break through Constance's haze of lust, and Alex's haze of consternation. Two heads whipped in his direction. Two identical looks of horror studied him for perhaps two heartbeats before they both scrambled guiltily to their feet.

"You brazen little pissant," Bronson roared, striding toward them with murder in his eye.

Alex gaped at him in horror, but quickly decided on the better part of valor. Whirling, she took off as fast as her feet could carry her, heading for the door at the back of the stables.

Constance shrieked as Bronson raced past her, throwing herself at him and catching him around one leg. Bronson hit the dirt hard enough it knocked the air from his lungs in a loud woof. Unfortunately, the shriek so traumatized Alex, her knees turned to water, and she tripped and rooted through a pile of hay.

The cursing behind her, as Bronson regained his feet, was enough to get her on her feet once more. She'd barely managed to cover half the distance, however, when something flew upon her, laying her out flat on her face in the middle of the pile of hay. As she struggled to rise, something landed upon the heavy boulder already weighing her down, and she realized Constance had arrived to the rescue even before she'd heard Constance's shriek, "Leave him alone, you bully!"

Bronson heaved upward, throwing his sister off. Stunned as she was by the impact of having both of them land on her, Alex knew her only chance of survival might be to run now while Constance held him off. Even as she struggled to her feet, however, Bronson reached out and grabbed her by one ankle, jerking her down again and clamping one ankle firmly between his thighs. Grabbing Constance by one arm, he dragged her across his lap and spanked her soundly.

She was still shrieking when he stopped and shoved her off his lap. "You, get to the house this instant while I deal with this cur, or I'll give you a beating you won't soon forget."

Rubbing her buttocks, Constance glanced from Bronson to Alex and finally whirled and fled.

Coward, Alex thought. "I swear, I never touched her!" she exclaimed when Bronson turned to her with blood in his eyes.

"Liar," Bronson growled, releasing his grip on Alex's ankle and turning to get to his feet.

The very moment he released her, Alex swung a kick directly at his face. She wasn't certain whether she was glad or sorry that she missed. It seemed doubtful that she would have stunned him, even if she'd managed to connect, and pretty nigh impossible that he could be angrier than he was at this moment.

Before she could do more than gape at him, he launched himself toward her, flattening her against the hay. Desperate to escape, but unable in her current position to throw an effective punch, Alex swung at him anyway, letting her blows fall where they might. A short tussle ensued while Bronson fought to catch hold of her flying fists, but in moments, he'd gripped both and borne them down into the hay on either side of her head.

For several heartbeats, they merely stared at each other, gasping for breath. Before Alex could think of anything that she might say that could possibly calm the situation, Bronson lowered his head, opening his mouth over hers in a kiss that shocked her to her toes.

Stunned, she didn't even think to breathe for several moments as his lips slanted over her own. Alex gasped in horror and outrage, and his tongue—his tongue—thrust into her mouth in a rough, possessive glide, filling her with the taste and feel of him. Alex's frightened, excited whimper seemed to increase his appetite, for he fair devoured her with his mouth like a starved beast. His fingers caressed her open palms, eliciting shivers as he swept his tongue through her crevices, touching and tasting with ravenous abandon.

A deep growl rumbled in Bronson's chest as he crushed down upon her, as if he wanted to sink into her flesh and meld to her bones. Alex moaned at the weight of him, the erotic glide of his tongue, the feel of his callused finger tips stroking her sensitive palms as if he wanted to touch -

more of her and would not. A hard knee parted her wanton thighs, pinning her ever harder to the ground, so close to her womanhood, she could scream with want of that heavy muscle against her most intimate parts.

Her veins felt flooded with liquid fire, her skin felt wondrously alive, highly sensitive to the slightest breath of movement. Heat suffused her belly, pooling in the crux of her thighs. Finally, when she thought she would expire from lack of breath and the sensation bursting for release inside her, he ceased the tender invasion.

Saints, she had not thought a man's mouth could create such pleasurable anticipation. Her body hungered for him.

Weak in the aftermath of his assault, it took an effort of will even to lift her eyelids when he released her hands finally and pulled away. Dreamily, she gazed up at him. Something about him did not seem quite right, however, and then it dawned on her.

Her mustache was stuck to his lip.

Her eyes widened in horror. Her mind went blank. It was only instinct that guided her as she jackknifed upright, hooked a hand around the back of his head, and kissed him firmly on the mouth in an effort to retrieve her lost disguise.

Gasps of revulsion immediately followed that clever recovery, and Alex drew back in surprise. It wasn't Bronson who'd uttered the gasps, however. It was his brothers, huddled behind them now, their expressions varying from plain shock, to shocked revulsion. Alex quickly checked her lip, thankful to find her mustache was back in place, even if a little crooked. She held her hand over her mouth as if in horror of … something….

"What is it?" her nemesis cried at their sounds of distaste. "Is he hurt? Is he dead? Tell me!"

Rafael grabbed Constance's shoulders and quickly shoved her back, placing his body between her and the scene behind him. "You don't want to see this. Believe me."

"Oh my god, he's killed him!"

"No, it's worse than that," Gray said, shuddering.

"Worse? Let me see," Constance cried, attempting to peer around the bulk of her two brothers to little avail.

With a growl of rage, Bronson rolled off of Alex, dragging her to her feet as he stood. Alex looked at Gray and Rafael, feeling herself color straight to her hairline. She wondered exactly how much they had seen….

"Are you all right, Bronson?" Gray asked a little doubtfully.

Bronson glared at him, shoved him out of the way, and stalked from the stable.

* * * *

With the barrier broken by Bronson's retreating backside, Constance slipped through the opening and rushed into Alex's arms. Alex grunted at the impact, patting her back in embarrassment before Constance pulled away and checked her for signs of injury or head trauma.

"How do you fair?" she asked as Alex pulled free and held her arms out to keep her at bay.

"I am well, dear lady, now that you have returned for help," Alex said, feeling her collar tighten about her throat. All this trouble, and she still had not managed to retrieve her horse. She doubted now that she would have a moment alone the remainder of her 'stay' with the Blackmores.

She absolutely refused to think about what Bronson had done to her. She found him to be the most attractive man she'd ever met. It horrified her to even consider that he could be attracted to her as she was now—a boy. Alex shuddered. What a tangle she had made of things.

"Constance, go now. We have matters to discuss with young Alex," Rafael said, crossing his arms over his chest in a manner that seemed most threatening to Alex.

"Not you as well, brothers!" Constance cried, hugging Alex protectively.

Alex struggled to breathe and fight her rising panic. She should be accustomed to this state by now, but she quite feared she would expire before she could free herself from their machinations. "'Twill be all right, Lady Constance. You must do as your brother says."

Reluctantly, Constance released her with a warning glare at her brothers as she strode out the door.

Gray and Rafael watched Alex, stone-faced, letting her feel their displeasure for long moments. Alex knew it was useless to do anything but await punishment. She was almost glad for it. A horrific sense of guilt permeated her. Her deception weighed heavily on her mind, for she feared what it's effect would have on the innocent, as well as herself.

Gray rubbed his face as though tired, running his fingers through his hair in a frustrated stroke. He gave her a hard look, as if trying to decide how best to broach what he wanted to say. Finally, he sighed and asked, "Alex, how long has it been since you've dipped your wick?"

Alex swallowed with difficulty past the heart which lodged in her throat. She was a horrid liar. She thought perhaps some measure of truth could aid her in her defense, though she knew not where this line of questioning could lead. With reluctance and a great deal of effort, she said, "I have never ... uh ... dipped my ... wick."

Gray and Rafael exchanged an unfathomable look with one another.

"It makes sense then," Gray admitted. "We must remedy your problem if you are to continue to stay here."

Alex's heart jumped and choked her. Surely not they too.... "I do not quite understand."

Rafael leaned one shoulder against a support beam. "'Tis simple. You would not be ... confused about your ... preferences if you'd had your coddles waxed."

Alex's head began to swim dizzily as blood rushed up her face. Certes! They meant to ... to ... she shuddered with horror and embarrassment. She could not do what they wanted her to. "No, no. That is not necessary," she hedged, wishing a bolt of lightning would strike her down rather than have this conversation with the men.

"It is necessary. We will not have our brother ruined by your seductions," Gray said, frowning as he came forward and closed a hand around her biceps.

She was beginning to feel a faint coming on, her breath was coming so fast and hard. Rafael surged forward and clapped her on the back with a grin. He had every appearance of being excited. In fact, they both looked over eager.

"Calm down, boy," Rafael said, guiding her out of the stable. "There really is naught to it. We shall find you an experienced whore for your first time."

Chapter Ten

Alex felt like a hen being chased for a stew. She had to escape. Unfortunately, between Gray and Rafael taking turns keeping an eye on her and Constance's concerns, she'd had not a moment alone the remainder of the day. By the evening meal, she was worn down to one frazzled nerve. She knew tonight Gray and Rafael planned to alleviate her 'malady', and she still had not thought of an excuse she could give to get out of it. It seemed she was destined to lose her virginity to a prostitute.

Thinking of carnal pleasures immediately brought Bronson to mind, and she wondered where he was. She had not seen him since the incident. He had not even come in for the evening meal, and she wondered if he was struggling with his feelings over what he'd done—and what she'd done. She blushed thinking of how she'd returned his kiss, even if only on the pretense of regaining her mustache—which was firmly pasted back into place. She longed to tell him he need not worry over his masculinity, that she was a woman, full grown and eager for the marriage bed in necessity and desire. Her courage was not so great, however, nor could she begin to imagine where he might have stormed off to or how long he would remain unseen.

It was as the servants were bringing out tureens of steaming water for cleansing that Bronson came into the dining hall. It fair stole her breath to see his long, powerful strides and the fluid movement of his body in motion. She hurt to look upon him, in that same achy place as before that throbbed to life whenever he was near. He should not have affected her thusly, but if naught else, she should have the ability to restrain her physical desires. That she could not refrain from experiencing a thrill on seeing him boded ill for her continued ease of mind.

He did not spare her a look as he seated himself beside his father and Rafael, but as he sat, he seemed to sense her eyes upon him and gifted her with a heated, angry look. He was persistent in his anger, and had been since her arrival. When first she'd met him, she felt like a mewling hound that merely annoyed him. In the past week, however, he'd seemed changed, more attune to her movements in the castle and on the grounds. She felt that he watched her always, even when she could not see him. Pure nonsense, she was certain. He'd even begun stealing into her dreams....

As he refused to break his angry look from her, Alex flushed to her hairline and glanced down at the platter a servant set before her.

That infallible look confirmed her suspicions. He was angry at her, and with good reason. If she was to gain another chance to escape, she would have to appease him somehow. She supposed the easiest course would be to apologize, even if the fault had not been entirely her own.

The meal was miserable for her. Each time she looked up, she would catch a look from one of the Blackmores. Constance batted her lashes at her, ever smiling, and her father, Lord Derwin, seemed oblivious to the turmoil that surrounded him. In fact, he almost looked encouraging to Constance, but Alex knew that had to be her overactive imagination playing tricks upon her eyes.

She could hardly bear to tear her eyes away from her meal, little though she ate. Gray and Rafael intercepted every look with a smile at what was to come, and Bronson fair hunkered down as he ate, growling at any who attempted conversation, looking like nothing so much as a beast.

Alex attempted to eat, but her throat closed on her food, and she could barely swallow in her anxiety. Her choking drew concern she did not want, and so she merely pushed her food about her plate until the entertainment began. She did not have long to wait until her doom, and she still had not thought of a way to escape Gray's and Rafael's clutches.

With morbid thoughts, she watched as a lutanist came in and sat upon the bottom step of the dais, strumming a tune as the gathering feasted.

The music appeared to agitate Bronson. He stood abruptly, scraping his chair as he strode out of the room. Alex waited a moment until she was certain the attention of the gathering had redirected to the lutist, and she slipped out, following him.

She had to speak to him of what had happened while she had the chance. Alex caught him on the stairs. His pace had slowed, almost as though he meant for her to capture him there as he ascended.

"My lord," she called, near breathless from her race to catch him.

He stopped on the stairs as if struck in the back by a bolt. He turned as she neared, his body rigid, his look unreadable.

"What do you want?" he asked in a stony voice that sent shivers down her spine.

Now that she had his attention, she was not certain she'd made a wise choice in gaining it. "I meant to speak to you … of what happened this day."

He frowned, and his heavy brows drew down like a thundercloud upon his forehead. Alex swallowed with difficulty, her mouth suddenly drawn free of moisture.

"What of it?" Bronson said through gritted teeth, stepping down until he was level with her on the wide tread. Her heart began pounding with a thrilling rush. Alex instinctively took a step down, but it leant him advantage over her that did not sit well.

"I mean to…" Alex began, swallowing again

as he took another step down, "...to apologize for my behavior."

He quirked a brow, crossing his arms over his chest. "You are at fault."

His words seemed more a question than statement, by the tone of his voice. "Aye," she said.

Bronson took another step, below her, cutting off escape as he leveled himself with her. Eye to eye with him now, Alex could not miss the heated intensity of his gaze. "I do as I wish. No one forces my will."

Alex frowned, fighting panic and confusion. "I … I do not catch your meaning, my lord—"

"Bronson," he growled, grabbing her arms and hauling her against his chest in the space of a frightened heartbeat. He captured her, complete and absolute, demanding surrender, and when she would not capitulate, he took it. He slanted his head, crushing his lips against hers, his mouth a brand that lit her blood on fire and commanded her submission.

Alex's heart leapt in her chest and galloped away. She was too stunned even to attempt to pull free. Her precarious position allowed her no retreat from him, and she knew not if she was more terrified of tumbling down the stairs, or being caught by a passerby with his arms about her.

As his arms tightened and his mouth opened, her mind closed down to her surroundings. Alex tasted the fury in his kiss, the absolute longing for sustenance. He seemed starved for the taste of her. He groaned against her lips, startling her as his tongue swept across the seam of her mouth and forged inside. Alex gasped at the hot taste of him, the unyielding press of his body around her. Small noises escaped from her throat, like the frightened pleas of prey. His arms tightened at the sound—they seemed to incite him. His tongue grew ravenous, his hands roaming her backside, squeezing the cheeks of her buttocks as he pulled her tight to his groin.

Alex moaned as his hardness ground against her belly. Wetness flooded her femininity, soaking her with forbidden arousal. Her blood felt on fire, her flesh achy with awakening desire. The wine on his tongue intoxicated her, made her forget he thought her a boy. She kissed him back, entangled her tongue with his in a bold move that left her thighs wet with her daring.

He groaned with approval as she advanced and tasted him. He suckled her tongue in his mouth, fingers massaging her cheeks, spreading them as he crushed her against him. The bud hidden in her folds throbbed to life, ached for his touch. She felt like crying out in frustration, wanted to wrap her legs around him and ease the hurt clenching her insides in a vice.

"Bronson," a deep, angry voice called behind them.

Bronson released her like he'd been struck with a brand. The suddenness of his withdrawal hit her with a force that stole her breath. Bronson faced the voice's owner—Gray—with a murderous look. His chest visibly rose and fell with his harsh breath. "Why do you interrupt, brother?" he ground out, his hands clenching as though he wanted to strangle something.

Alex watched them both, eager to flee but rooted in place. She shuddered, hugging herself. She would have claimed innocence of wrongdoing, but knew they would not believe her. She couldn't seem to work her tongue, regardless. Her lips felt bruised from his kiss, tingled with the lingering pressure of his mouth, and her blood raced, making her lightheaded. She placed a hand on her heart, unsure if it would continue to beat with the shocks she'd been gifted this day.

Gray propped on the bottom step. "Be glad Rafael intercepted father. Do you want him to see you this way? Do you want Constance to?"

Guilt assailed her. Her apology lay like ash in her mouth, burned away by the molten fire of his tongue. She could not see reason when faced with Bronson. His presence addled her wits, made her careless. It was pure miracle that they continued to believe her a boy, but then, they were too concerned with Bronson's soul to consider other possibilities.

And Bronson … he seemed not to care, either way.

Bronson shuddered, raking a frustrated hand through his hair. Alex longed to ease the worry on his brow, the tension in his muscles, but she didn't dare move and draw attention to herself. The men felt on edge, as if one wrong turn would set them on a irreversible, dangerous course.

Bronson turned away without a word, giving Alex a last, heated look before he trod up the stairs in angry silence.

After he'd disappeared from view, Gray came up, grasped her arm, and pulled her down the stairs with a scowl. "Were you more than a child and capable of withstanding it, I would beat you, young lord, for tempting my brother in sin. His will is weakened from want of woman flesh, and you are too comely by far for his mind to seek ease. A serpent cares not which hole it sleeps in."

Rafael ran up to them from a branching hall as they came off the stairs. He gave Alex a look, as well as Gray's hand upon her arm, before turning his attention to his brother. "All is well, Gray?"

"I came none too soon. Young Alex is too curious by far to feel Bronson's serpent climb up his arse," Gray said with a scowl.

"Then it is good we go bawding this night. I have had the horses prepared. Naught stands in our way but the road."

Alex felt faint. Her feet tripped over themselves, and Gray barely righted her. Her blood seemed to boil. She would have placed a hand to her head to feel for fever, but Rafael grabbed her free arm to escort her outside to the stables.

She was gone to her doom and there was naught to stop it.

* * * *

The old battlements were tranquil this night, allowing Bronson reprieve from the company of others and opportunity to allow his blood to cool. Flames whipped in a cool breeze, ruffling like sails filled with air in the quiet. The landscape was dark, and he followed the movement of torch

116

bearing riders as they crossed the creek and rode to their own homes. He did not puzzle over their lingering at the castle overlong. He breathed deeply, forcing himself to relax, pacing the battlements as though it would clear his thoughts the more he walked. He came here when troubled, and indeed, the girl toyed with the calm of his mind like no other.

Long moments passed, and still, the sensation of her in his grasp did not abate. His flesh felt imprinted with the touch of her.

He could still smell her scent, impressed on his skin. His hands burned with the feel of her buttocks, round and firm, each cheek sized to suit the length and width of his hands like he was meant to hold her. He'd felt her arousal seeping through his hose, and he'd near gone mad with it, imagining the scent, the taste, how it would feel to plunge his engorged length into her silky wet depths.

He groaned, increasing the arousal that tormented him. Bronson felt near to bursting. His groin throbbed with the heavy beat of his heart, aching like a starved beast. He felt like a man possessed by some demon, intent on rending and ravishment.

Carnal thoughts did nothing to ease the turmoil of his mind—they merely enhanced it. He would gain no surcease if he did not turn them from the temptation of her woman's sheath.

Still, the mystery of her presence eluded his probing. He'd gained no information from her thrusting his tongue into her mouth, and yet, he could not resist claiming her as his own, no matter what his brothers thought.

The girl … she must think him a monster. He behaved as one, unthinking, demanding, rough and intent on bedding her. How much did she know of men's ways? Had she come to him tonight merely to apologize? It did not seem likely. It seemed more a covert act disguised with boldness, some intent to cause him ruin, though he knew not the reason if that was the case.

He didn't want to believe it, but he had to keep such thoughts present, else he would indeed risk ruination.

"My lord," a servant called from behind him, breathless from running up the stairs.

Bronson faced him, scowling at the interruption on his thoughts. "What is it?" he asked tersely.

The man stopped before him, holding a missive. "A messenger carried this, directing it to your attention."

Bronson took it, unrolling the parchment and angling it toward the torch light.

Lord Bronson Blackmore,

You have refused our messengers and missives this week past. This is my final offer for peaceable negotiations. I ask again, return the girl tonight. Your failure to comply will necessitate our clan to reclaim her by force.

Hugh McPherson, Laird of the Clan McPherson

Bronson crumpled the paper in his fist and threw it to the stone floor. It was confirmed. The girl was, without doubt, a McPherson, but from the tone of the letter, they thought he held her captive. He could not fathom why they would think that, unless she had been scheduled to report back to them and missed her appointment. It made sense.

He was disgusted with himself and their defenses for allowing a spy in their midst, for allowing lust to overrule his senses. He did not know why the McPhersons would do this, nor did he care.

He would not easily give her up. Now that the time had come that he could, and should, he was loath to release her from his sight. What's more, what information had she gleaned from their household? No, it would not do to give her over to them and spill their secrets. "Where is Lord Montague?" he asked the waiting servant.

The man blanched at Bronson's black look, looking as though he would bolt, or faint, at any moment. "He … he is g-gone, my lord."

"What?" Bronson roared, feeling blinding panic clutch his chest in a vice. "Where has he gone?" he demanded angrily, annoyed that the man didn't immediately respond.

The servant blinked rapidly, clutching his heart. "He … he is with your brothers, my lord. They ventured to The Bristle Boar an hour past…."

Bronson listened no more—there was no need to once their destination had spilled from the man's lips. He rushed past the gaping servant down the stairs leading into the castle, impotent fury building inside him with every ground eating stride. He tried not to think of what they had done, what danger they were in ... what danger Alex was in from every direction. He strode through the belly of the castle and out to the grounds where he saddled his horse himself, too impatient to wait for a groomsman. Through every terse move, every breath, the image of them moving closer to doom bade his mind roil with frustration and anger.

There was only one reason he could think of why Gray and Rafael would tow Alex off and go to The Bristle Boar at this hour. He knew his brothers, knew they'd seen him with Alex. He was not grateful for their interference, and would not divulge his knowledge to them. It should be enough that his life was his own, not theirs, but it was not.

Bronson seethed with outrage and the unwitting error of their course. He prayed he would get to them in time to prevent their folly.

If the McPhersons did not set upon them as they left and slaughter the lot of them, Bronson would strangle his brothers when he arrived at the alehouse.

Chapter Eleven

Rafael and Gray tossed their arms to the gay sounds of music and merrymaking around them, singing along with a bawdy tune, sloshing their mugs as they danced in their chairs and tightened their arms around wenches kissing each one's neck and chest. Every now and then they would pinch the backside of a passing maid to catch her attention and refill their mugs. Alex had never seen such out and out decadence and mingling of the classes. If she wasn't so horrified, she might have been impressed that their differences in stature made no difference at all.

As it was, she could hardly think or breathe for the scent of unwashed men, stale beer, and a badly smoking fire that left a haze through the room that trapped the repulsive odors exquisitely.

Catching her ill look, Gray smiled and asked, "Alex, have you not found a wench to your liking? If you worry for coin, do not. It is my treat this night."

Alex shook her head, fighting the horror climbing over her. She'd tried very hard not to look at her surroundings. The Bristle Boar was stuffed as a Christmas goose with men drinking and groping eager women, whose dresses were slashed and trimmed to expose their breasts. On some of the more brazen maids, she'd even spied the dusky hue of their nipples. She expected any moment to see one lift her skirts and expose the lot of them.

Her face surely deepened to three shades of red, her embarrassment ran so deep.

"You dawdle overmuch, young Alex. Surely you would enjoy a fire-haired maiden? All men do," Rafael said, grinning as he dropped his mug and grabbed a passing barmaid. "Come, my lovely maiden. How fair you this even?"

The redhead made no attempt to pull free, but gave him a saucy smile, ignoring the scowl from the wench on his lap. "Right fine, milord. 'Ave you somethin' you wish o' me?"

"Aye, lovely, a matter of grave importance," Rafael said, his voice dropping as he glanced at Alex. "I've a youngling in need of rescue of his immortal soul. Might you be up to a challenge?"

Alex swallowed hard as the woman's gaze crept to her and climbed her, up and down, particularly lingering on her groin. "Aye, I can be—fer a price."

Gray grinned at her, setting his mug down as he dug into a pouch at his side. "But of course, fair maiden." He fished some gold out and laid it on the table. "I trust this will do."

The redhead's eyes widened with lust. She took the coin up, tucking it into her bodice as she sauntered around the table to where Alex sat. The girl sat on Alex's lap without prompting, threw her arms around her neck, and planted a messy, wet kiss on her lips.

Alex sputtered and pushed the girl back. The girl gave her a confused look, then looked back at the brothers. "What the 'ell? 'E got somethin' wrong wit 'im?"

"The poor lad has never had his coddles waxed. You'll be his first. A special honor, it is, to be sure. I trust you can be … gentle?" Gray asked with a wink and a smirk.

"We've paid for a room upstairs—the usual," Rafael said, giving her directions to it.

The girl pulled Alex up, holding her arm with unnatural strength as she guided her up the stairs to the rooms above. Alex felt a mounting dread crawling through her mind. The girl seemed eager to perform her duty and keep the coin.

They were inside the room before Alex scarce knew what happened. A bed built with gnarled, aging wood stood against one corner. A small table stood beside it, holding a crock of some substance and a flickering candle. It was a dark room—mayhap the girl would never notice….

The maid closed the door behind her, startling Alex from her morbid stillness. Alex whirled around, faced with the smiling bawd.

"Do ye prefer your gels bare arsed or clothed, milord?"

123

Removing her clothes would give her more time, but Alex simply could not bear the thought of looking on a naked woman and having her hands on her as well. "Clothed," she said hoarsely.

She advanced on Alex, swaying her hips.

"W-what is it you're called?" Alex asked, stalling, backing away.

"Everyone calls me Red, milord. Yer a true gentleman fer askin' me name. Now," —she pushed on Alex's chest, upsetting her balance— "sit here." Alex fell back, collapsing on the bed. She struggled back upright, swallowing convulsively.

"We need a bit o' grease for this, lovey," she murmured as she knelt between Alex's knees and picked up the jar from the bedside table. A whiff of pungent, solidified oil assailed her nostrils as the girl passed it over her knees and dipped two fingers inside, scooping out the lubrication. She planted her other hand on Alex's thigh, sliding it up toward where her cock should be.

Self-preservation kicked to the forefront. Alex put her hand over the woman's, holding it still. "Please, madam, I am not prepared," she said, her voice just shy of a shriek.

Red grinned, looking unperturbed. "Ye will be when I slick this on yer manroot."

The door suddenly slammed open like it had been hit by a gale wind. Bronson stormed in as if he'd been thrown, and looked around the room with fury gleaming in his eyes. The girl jumped to her feet, gaping at Bronson. Alex's jaw dropped.

Bronson pointed at the woman. "You, out."

Red scurried past him with the cringing movement of someone expecting a beating. Bronson ignored the woman, and slammed the door shut behind her as she left, turning the lock on the door before facing Alex yet again.

Alex's relief at being rescued from certain exposure was short lived as Bronson crossed the room in two short, swift strides, grasped her arms, and hauled her onto her feet. Her body bounded against his chest, stilled by the strength of his hands and the steel of his grip. Her breath caught in her lungs at his smoky, angry look. He gave her a slight shake as she continued to gape up at him.

"What mean you by coming here?" he asked, his eyes dark and unforgiving. "Was this mine brothers' idea or your own?"

Through strength of will she'd not known she possessed, Alex fought back the rising tide of fright and excitement and found her voice. "'Twas your brothers, my lor—Bronson," she stammered.

"Are you not over young to know the pleasures of the flesh?" His hands tightened on her arms. His jaw clenched with his anger, making her ache in secret places as she followed the hard line to his sensual lips. She feared he would kiss her—she feared he would not. She almost preferred a beating to this everlasting torment and the indecision that gripped her whenever he was near. Her body responded to his presence as though it possessed a separate mind, willing and eager to know the full extent of these sins of the flesh.

Alex shook her head, trying to make sense of him and the direction his thoughts lay. Why would he be angry at her for his brother's action, unless he truly wanted to possess her himself. The thought, which should have dismayed her, thrilled her instead. "Nay. I am full grown. You know this."

"I know nothing but what you tell me," he bit out as if pained.

"'Tis the truth. Your brothers brought me here so that I would … that I could…." Certes, she could not tell him they sought to assuage her appetite for his sex.

"They think you aim to seduce me," he said with a growl, his voice dropping to a husky murmur that rubbed along her nerves. "Do you?"

"Nay," she whispered, flushing with the heat of his eyes as he dragged his gaze down her face and throat. Her breasts swelled as her desire soared. The bindings had never before felt so painful.

"Whether you willed it or no, you have succeeded," he said, anger heating his voice. He bent his head and covered her lips, plunging her into instant, desperate hunger.

Her mouth opened of its own accord, allowing him inside, sucking his tongue as it plunged deep into her mouth. He groaned into her, tasting her essence even as she drank his with abandon. He stole her breath, her will to fight. The sanity of her mind burned away under the molten glide of his tongue in and out of her mouth. She was mad, mad to allow this, to not struggle in his arms and break away.

126

He tore from her suddenly, shocking her to stillness, turning her around and pushing her against the wall at the foot of the bed. She planted her palms on the surface to cushion herself, jerking in surprise as the wood cooled her feverish skin. An astonished gasp escaped her throat as he nipped the back of her neck, branding her with his lips, marking a trail around to her ear. She leaned her head back, trying to get closer, trembling as the wet swath of his tongue cut a shivering path round her neck.

He crowded her against the wall, forcing her to lay her cheek on it as he slipped his hands over her wrists and pinned them to the wall. He ground his groin into the cleft of her buttocks, sudden and hard. She moaned at the forceful push, gasping at the feel of his cod piece digging against that most intimate part of her. Wetness bloomed between her thighs, leaving her uncomfortably aware of how much he affected her.

A frustrated groan rumbled from his lips against her neck as he ground into her again, building that ache inside her. He clamped her wrists together with one massive hand, easing the pressure on her backside. She felt weak at the size of his hands, the strength he used to bend her to his will. His domination would be her undoing, and certes, she wanted it.

His sharp intake of breath against her neck made her shiver, and then he closed the finite distance once more. There was a change this time, from cold leather to hot flesh.

"I can show you the sins of flesh if you are

eager, Alex," he breathed against her neck, tickling the fine hairs on her flesh.

She shivered, wanting to say no, but wanting her exposure, wanting to know what it would feel like to have his manflesh deep inside her. She said nothing, and her silence seemed to spur him on.

His hips shifted, rubbed against her. The rigid length of his manhood pressed into the thin linen that covered her buttocks. The short hose felt as nothing compared to the fire that radiated from his groin. With that same free hand, he dragged both layers of hose off her buttocks, allowing them to hang down on her thighs.

The barrier gone, he nudged his cock against the naked cleft of her buttocks, searching for a hole. Heat curled in her belly, erupted through her veins like molten lead.

"Long has this beast hungered for sustenance," he growled harshly against her ear, his breath teasing. "Can this sweet cleft appease its greed, I wonder?"

The sexual menace in his words turned her knees to water. She felt close to fainting with the desire whirling in her head. "There's naught to feed it, my lord," she whispered.

He grasped her and twisted, pushing her to the bed. She fell upon it, a surprised gasp escaping her as he came down on her from behind, between her legs. Oh God, no. She panted from excitement at what was to come, laying utterly still, digging her hands into the mattress. He would find her out now. She almost welcomed it.

The bed shook as he shifted his weight behind her, and a sharp scent drifted to her nostrils. Alex had no sooner recognized the pungent grease again, when she felt fingers spread her buttocks and a cold substance spread across her anus.

"What are you doing?" she cried, trying to raise up and twist away from him. One meaty hand held her in place, kept her from moving as a thick finger rang the rim and dipped suddenly inside, carrying with it the slick substance.

She moaned at the invasion, jerking with surprise as he stretched her, working the lubrication inside her tight hole. Could it be he still did not realize who she was, that he'd not seen her woman's sheath or the lack of a manroot? He curled inside her, probing, and her womb clenched with a tremor of pleasure, wiping all thought from her mind.

He grunted with approval, slipping another finger inside her, stretching her more than she'd thought imaginable. The inner muscles of her anus clenched on him, the pressure easing as he stroked inside and out.

He withdrew his hands as she relaxed to the feel of him. She smelled more grease, and then he leaned over and urged her to her knees. He grasped her hips, bringing her back against him. Something prodded her rear hole, pushing, pushing, moving inward with slow, inexorable deliberation. Alex whimpered, digging her hands into the bed as fire erupted along the tender rear muscles.

Bronson groaned, relentlessly forcing his way

129

inside her slick anus, coated with the grease that would soothe his passage. Her muscles gripped him like a vice, resistant to his invasion. She squirmed her bottom against his hips, near to undoing him.

He grit his teeth, sweat popping along his upper lip, dampening his hair as he pushed forward, past the fragile outer muscles and deep into the core of her anus. She cried out as he sank to the hilt in her, grinding her rounded cheeks against his groin.

Bronson held still, reveling in the agony that gripped his cock like a silken hand. Her inner muscles quaked, clenching and unclenching on his shaft, urging him to move, to ram deeper inside her again and again.

More than anything, he wanted to touch her slit, slip his fingers into her sheath and make her scream in ecstasy. The bud in her folds beckoned his touch. He smelled her arousal oozing down her exposed thighs. It took an inhuman strength not to withdraw from her rear hole and pound into her sheath. He knew she would be blissfully tight, that her juices would fire the pleasure aching to burst from his loins.

His mouth watered at the thought of tasting her honeyed cream. He wanted to nibble her breasts, and he wondered quite suddenly of the shade of her nipples and how dusky her folds. Did they swell for him, quiver for his touch?

He could take no more—his cock bade him move, to drive into her. He dug his fingers into her hips, holding her still as he slid his shaft from her hole, inch by inch. She was crying, though whether in pleasure or pain, he could not know.

"Do you wish it to stop?" he gritted out, his breath heaving in his lungs from the exertion of maintaining control.

"Please," she whimpered, arching her back. "I must have … something…."

The pleading in her voice was his undoing. He plunged into her again, feeling as though he would die from the tight clench of her muscles, the gasps that tore from her throat. He set a pace, his groin erupting in bursts of pain that bordered on pleasure, hammering into her, shaping her to the length and breadth of his cock.

He stretched her until Alex thought her flesh would tear asunder. His cock was unbelievably large, and the bulb on the tip elicited tingles of achy pleasure throughout her entirety. Her womb contracted at the nearness of his shaft, tremulous pleasure piercing her belly in waves.

It was all Alex could do to keep from collapsing as he slammed against her, into her. Her buttocks were on fire, pain and pleasure mingling in an intoxicating mix that rushed through her veins and left her drunk with arousal. She heard the slap of his coddles against the narrow band of flesh that separated her entrances, found the smacking sound and his groans of pleasure only heightened her own arousal. She should not want this sinful intrusion. She should not grind against him, searching, seeking some thing.

The sensation neared her as he rocked inside her, increasing his tempo until her arms shook with the forceful invasion. He seemed beyond controlling himself, beyond thought of anything but the steady movement.

Something neared, a sensation that vibrated along her very fiber, made her want to curl up with it, stretch and reach, desperately climbing. Inexorably, it moved, creeping into the bud hidden in her folds and the clench of muscles in her femininity.

She felt close to it, almost close enough she could grasp it. A ragged cry behind her tore the feeling away as he thrust a final time inside her. His shaft rippled, spurting a hot fluid deep inside her. The heat made her toes and fingers curl, caused her muscles to twitch in response, yet that sensation she was so eager for eluded her. He emptied his seed inside her tight hole and withdrew roughly. She felt his shudder against her buttocks and knew he'd found some sort of fulfillment she had not.

Bronson collapsed on the bed beside her, dragging her down to lay against him. She curled into his chest, enjoying the heat of him, his hands stroking her back. She steadfastly ignored the ache between her thighs and her enjoyment of his sensual invasion.

"I never knew the pleasure to be found with one such as you," he murmured against her forehead.

Alex stiffened, horror assailing her. Dear Saints above! After everything he'd done, he still thought her a boy. Alex felt sick with her deceit, sick with the knowledge that she'd turned him somehow.

She knew not what she could do to resolve this, and her heart ached to know that he might never want her in her true guise.

Her troubles with the king and pending marriage seemed faraway now, lost to the feel of Bronson's loving and the brand of his mouth and manroot. Would she ever be able to correct this matter? She feared not. She knew it shouldn't matter. He was an enemy of her family. She could only imagine what they would think if they knew how close she'd come to the enemy—rather, how much he'd invaded her intimacies. She was ruined, either way.

"Time wastes. We needs must be on our way before the hour grows too late. Mine brothers must surely know what we've done. There will be no appeasing them now."

Alarm made her bolt upright and free herself from his arms. "Will they slay me for trespass?"

He smiled at her, looking infinitely younger and carefree. He'd changed somehow. Alex bit her lip, fighting back her fears. "They will do nothing so long as I live, I promise you that, Alex."

"You said yourself they thought I meant to seduce you."

His mouth quirked in a beguiling half-smile as he laid his head on one arm, bent as a pillow 'neath him. "And so you have."

"'Twas not all my doing."

"Nay. A devil possesses me. I thought never to lay hands on a boy, but you seem more woman than manchild."

Blood rushed her face. She tried to stammer

133

out a reply, but could think of nothing to say.

"Do I offend your manhood, Alex?"

"Nay, it could never be so," she said wryly.

"I thought as much. Mayhap from this point forward, we can begin to explore this new side of ourselves."

Alex could feel a faint coming on. This deception would never last. More than ever, she had to be free. She'd created a monster in Bronson. Now she had two Blackmores eager for her tail, both Bronson and Constance. The hunt would like as not fell her. She was suddenly exhausted. All burgeoning pleasure had fled her, and she wanted nothing more than to be alone, in her room and in her bed—if they could subsist for so brief a time.

"Your lips distract me," he murmured, heatedly watching her chew her bottom lip. "If we do not go now, I fear we shall not leave this night."

Alex swallowed with difficulty. She scooted off the bed, dragging her long and short hose up over her buttocks miserably before he could see her nakedness. She felt sticky with her arousal and his seed, and knew she must wash soon, or she would be in agony for hours with the reminder of his claiming.

Instead of the warm feeling she'd had before, she was cold now, for it served as nothing else but reinforcement that she did not belong with the Blackmores, nor ever would.

Chapter Twelve

Bronson did not come to her as he threatened, to begin an illicit affair 'neath the noses of his kin, for which she was eternally grateful. If she'd seen him again, she knew she could not go through with her plan to escape.

All the night, she tossed and turned, dreaming up ways to flee the Blackmore household. Finally, before exhaustion claimed her, she lit upon a plan that excited her, and brought forcibly home how little she'd paid attention to her surroundings.

On her first night at Derwin Hall, the McPhersons had raided. Many were on foot it seemed. In fact, she couldn't remember seeing their horses, but regardless of whether or not they'd had means of transportation, the fact remained that they must be within a distance she could reasonably expect to walk to within a few day's time.

She felt a thousand kinds of fool for not realizing such a simple truth sooner. She didn't dare go to the stables again—that was expected of her. However, she didn't believe any among them would suspect she would just walk away.

It was a perfect plan. Armed with it, she would succeed. She slept well into the next day, easing the aches that plagued her mind and body. She kept to her room most of the day, leaving only to partake of the communal meals.

As dusk gathered, she realized Bronson was avoiding her, as were his brothers. She smiled to herself, thinking of how horrified they must surely be at her actions. They deserved it.

With dark upon her, she made ready to enact her plan. She waited until the dwindling moon rose in the sky, and then she crept through the quiet household, holding her breath as she listened for movement or sound of discovery.

It remained quiet even as she stole outside and gathered her bearings, moving in the direction where the raid had taken place. She felt certain her cousins must live that way, and even if they did not, it could be her fortune would improve and she'd happen upon another raid.

She could always hope.

As much light as the moon shed, it still wasn't enough to completely reveal the ground to her. She was not so foolhardy as to bring a torch, and so she walked slowly, carefully, feeling the ground with each step to make certain she did not injure herself.

Before long, she completely lost sight of the castle. Her heart jumped for joy. She would succeed in this.

* * * *

"My lord," a voice whispered loudly, rousing Bronson from his slumber. He came up with a growl, scowling at the person who'd disturbed him. Blinking in the dimness as watered light crept through his window, he saw it was the maid, Elizabeth, who'd come into his room.

For a moment, he tried to remember why she would enter his room, and then he remembered—he'd set her to watching Alex.

Alarm seized him. "Aye? What is it? What has happened?"

"My lord, I-I am sorry for awaking you, but you bade me come if I saw Lord Montague on the grounds."

"What is it? Is he attempting to leave?" he asked as he threw his legs over the edge of the bed and stood, staggering toward his chest so that he could dress.

"Nay, my lord," she responded, looking at him worriedly, averting her eyes from his nakedness.

"Then what is it?" he asked impatiently as he pulled a shirt on and followed it with a short tunic.

"He has already gone."

"What?" he demanded, facing her with a thunderous look. His gut clenched with sudden pain.

"I am sorry, my lord," she cried, coming to her knees before him. She grasped the front of his tunic. "I fell asleep on my post. When I

137

awakened and went to Lord Montague's room to stir the fire, I found he'd gone. I-I searched the grounds and could not find him. His horse is still in the stables. I had not thought he would go without his horse. Please, forgive me, my lord, for failing you."

Bronson bent and peeled her hands from his tunic, fighting the pain that held him in its grip. With effort, he said, "The fault is mine own. Pray, do not cry, good woman. I cannot bear a woman's tears."

She sniffled, standing shakily with his assistance.

"It is good you came to me when you did. Now, go to the stablemaster and bid him prepare Ebony for travel. I expect it to be done when I come down."

"I will, my lord," she said, backing out of the room.

Bronson angrily pulled on his doublet and hose and fastened his cod piece in place. He was furious with himself and Alex. He'd pushed too far. He knew he should not have bedded her, not in that way. She was a maiden, and he'd taken her in a way no maiden should ever been taken. No matter how much he wanted to bed her, he should have resisted his base instincts. But the sight of her with that whore between her legs had enflamed him, and she'd looked up at him, not with fear in her eyes, but hope and relief.

He'd ignored that look as his blood fled to his cock. All he'd been able to think about was her spread legs, her soft lips that begged for his kisses.

He was little more than a rutting madman. It was no wonder she acted much of the time as if she were in a terror. Bronson cursed his monstrous behavior.

Now she had fled, gone back to the kin that demanded her return.

Was he too late to take her back? Had the McPhersons lain in wait, taken her while he slept? It was entirely likely that she had been, and still, he could not help the fragile hope that clung to him and begged him make haste.

His shoes on, his sheathed sword strapped in place, he rushed out of his room, downstairs and out onto the grounds. The household was barely alive at the ungodly hour. His brothers would offer no help or hindrance—he was on his own.

Bronson prayed that she had only just gone. He had no notion of what path she'd taken, but he would travel the most direct route to the McPhersons and hope she'd not had the fore-thought to cover her tracks. She was on foot. With luck, he could easily catch up to her. If her kin found her first, however, he would have a fight on his hands, and though blows had never been fatal before, he could not imagine that they would continue to be so, not when they were so desper-ate to get her back.

The stablemaster held Ebony's reigns out to him as he came out, and Bronson swung up into the horse's saddle, digging his heels into the horses flanks and racing out to find the woman who'd escaped him.

He would find her. When he did, she would

beg for forgiveness.

Bronson tore through the countryside, the landscape coming alive as the sun crept over the horizon. Ebony snorted with the effort, his hooves eating the ground. Bronson cast about, searching his surroundings for some sign of her passing. He could see nothing, and as he drew near the pastures where their cattle was kept and beyond, his hope dwindled.

Cresting the rise of a small hill, Bronson slowed to a stop, guiding Ebony along the swell and looking about from his vantage point. He spied the blocky shapes of cattle, their heads to the ground as they leisurely ate. To the East lay forest, and to the West, more green land turning brown with the coming winter.

He was surprised the little fool hadn't frozen to death in the cold of the night, but it was a fair day despite the time of year, and she was a stubborn little thing.

Bronson sighed, rubbing his tired eyes, tightening his knees on Ebony as she sidled. The sun was glaring down now, he felt the heat of it on his hair.

He sighed again, in frustrated anger. She was gone. He'd let her slip through his fingers. Either her kin had taken her as soon as she'd left, or she'd followed another path. It hardly mattered now, either way.

As he pulled on the reigns to turn Ebony, movement caught the corner of his eye. He stopped, staring hard to the distance. Moving between the cattle was a man, slight in stature and build, dressed in a black doublet and hose. What drew his attention was the faint swath of red from the slashed sleeves and the flip of a cape as the wind caught it.

Why had he been blind to her before? He'd not even searched amongst the cattle for her. He'd been so certain she was gone, he'd grown slack and unseeing. Cursing his carelessness, Bronson kicked Ebony's flanks, descending the hill at a breakneck pace, his quarry in sight.

* * * *

Alex heard the hooves before she saw the rider. At first she thought it a passerby, or mayhap her kin on a raid, and then she realized the sound of thunder came from behind her. She whirled around, sure the ground shook from the rider's pace. Her legs became unsteady, her knees wobbling as she saw who approached. Weakness flooded her in a debilitating wave.

Bronson!

Alex whirled back around, running. She was not going to stand still and let him capture her without trying to flee. He would have a fight on his hands. If nothing else, her pride would not allow her capitulation.

She struggled up the slight rise that stood in her way, her aching legs burning from the effort, her lungs fighting to drag air into her beleaguered body. Sweat beaded on her skin despite the stiff breeze ruffling her wig and cape. She shivered, ignoring the discomfort and the growing intensity of the hoof beats behind her. She heard the frightened lowing of the cattle, heard them flee just as she did. Her feet slipped on a dew slicked patch of grass, and her feet nearly went out from under her in two different directions.

The beats roared in her ears. She felt heat on her back, pushing her onward, harder, faster. Her lungs felt close to bursting, pain stabbed her ribs.

Suddenly she was flying, choking, her doublet close around her throat as she went sailing into the air, her arms and legs flailing, one half of her crossing over the breadth of the horse in a move that stunned her with its impossibility. She landed with a loud woof on a lap as hard and unyielding as iron. Instinctively, she wrapped her thighs tight against the heaving flanks of the horse to keep from falling off. She grasped the pommel for dear life as he turned his mount sharply and headed in the opposite direction.

One thick, heavily muscled arm came across her middle, pulling her flush against the rigidity of his chest. Alex screamed and clawed at the arm, her struggles ineffectual against the thickness of his sleeves.

"Cease, boy, I would not have you hurt us both," he ground out, tightening on her until she relented and gasped for breath.

Frustrated tears stung her eyes as she was forced to relax back against his chest. She tried to hold herself rigid, but fighting him exhausted her, and she was already weary from walking half the night. And to what purpose? He'd found her anyway, ignored her fighting and screaming and done what he willed.

She wasn't ready to cease her plans to escape.

He'd captured her this time, he would not do so again. She meant to continue her plans. Her very life depended upon seeing her cousins. The king's ire would soon grow to fury. She could not allow a fellow countryman to come under the blade. Her Scottish cousins were not bound by the king's law as they were. She half thought he deserved the punishment of their Sire.

"I wish to be free of you," Alex ground out, squirming in his hold. His mammoth of a horse had already swallowed the ground it had taken her half an hour to cross, already crossed the hill she'd had so much trouble both climbing and descending. It was a hopeless plan that she'd enacted—she saw that now. The only way for her to succeed would be to gain her own horse.

"Your will is at odds with mine own, and I am always the victor," he said, grunting as she elbowed him in the stomach and struggled anew.

"My will is as great," she bit off, wriggling in his lap. He was as hard as oak, and just as uncomfortable to sit upon. The heavy trot of the horse bounced her, forcing her to accept his hold when she wanted nothing more than to be free of his touch.

Her backside felt branded. His scent seeped into her pores. She hated smelling him, hated the weakness that assaulted her, made her want to give in and do nothing but wallow on his skin and absorb his heat and scent until she'd lost herself. She fought not only him, but her traitorous body as well. She felt like two halves, split asunder, one eager for his bedding, the other eager for freedom no matter the cost.

"Aye," he growled, capturing her attention as a snare, "it is your will that intrigues me. Cease your movement this instant or you will regret it!"

Alex clamped her mouth shut and wiggled again for pure spite. She wouldn't have dared if she'd known what his response would be. With a ragged groan, he pulled recklessly hard on the reigns, making the horse rear. Bronson lifted his leg to the rear and dropped down on the ground, pulling her unceremoniously from the saddle.

Before she could think to scream, he brought her tumbling to the ground, rolling on top of her, crushing the wind from her lungs. "You tempt me more than words can say. I should spank you for the trouble you cause," he bit out as he covered her lips with his own and drove his hard body between her legs.

Alex cried out into his mouth at the forceful grind against her cleft, low, toward her buttocks. She pushed at his shoulders, trying to fight him off, horrified at his sensual intent. They were in the open, for any and all to see. He fought her hands off him, struggled to capture her wrists and pin them above her head as he dragged his mouth along the line of her jaw.

He hadn't shaved. He must have come directly from waking. A thrill arched through her at the thought of him tearing from bed to come for her. Her skin felt afire with the rough abrasion of his shadowy whiskers, the brand of his lips trailing along to her ear.

"You left before my serpent supped, sweet

Alex," he murmured hot against her ear, dragging her lobe between his teeth. He thrust his hips against her as if to prove his point.

Alex shuddered, her arms tense as she strove to break his hold. "The dining hall is closed, my lord," she grit out, clamping her legs against his hips, planting her feet on the ground. She arched her back, trying to buck him off.

Laughter rumbled from his chest. His breath fanned the heat swarming her veins. "I believe there is a bite to be had."

He released her briefly, only to grasp her hose and drag it from under her, rounding the curve of her buttocks until they lay bare on the grass. Alex gasped in shock, reaching for her hose even as she stopped in disbelief as he untied the cod piece and revealed his manroot to her. It stood from the white hose in stark contrast, flesh red and angry, blue hewn veins engorged with blood. His cock looked every inch the ravaging beast, intent on its dinner. She was horrified and fascinated all at once.

He reached on either side of him, locking his hands around her ankles, hauling them around before his chest. Alex tried to kick him, but his grip was unbreakable. He looked down at her, his hair wild around his shoulders and forehead, his eyes feverish and dark. He looked at her beneath hooded lids, heavy with lust.

Alex dug into the dirt, jerking as he pushed forward and down, trapping her legs between their bodies. The position stretched her uncomfortably as her knees touched her chest, and she felt cool fingers of air slip across her buttocks just before the blistering prod of his cock head nudged her anus.

Her muscles clenched, refusing to give entrance. Holding her eyes, he took his palm and swathed it with his tongue. Alex shuddered as his hand moved down, out of sight, to his groin, and then she felt him push, felt the delicate muscles of her anus stretch to accommodate his rigid flesh. His saliva felt cool, little lubrication for so tight a place.

He pushed past the inner muscles, to the hollow core of her waiting for his possession. He closed his eyes, arching his head back as he sank inside. He stopped as the bulb of his shaft entered, then pulled back until he'd nearly receded, and thrust in again. His moves were short, allowing only the thick head to enter her.

Alex panted for breath, moaning as his pubic bone brushed against her trapped cleft. She longed to feel him inside that other place. Her nub ached, pulsing with the beat of her heart. Alex cried out as he pumped carefully inside her, never giving the release her body screamed for.

Fire seared her back entrance as he stroked, building her lust to a frightening crescendo. Desperate pleas tore from her throat, she was mad with the desire fogging her brain. She dug her hands into the ground, trying to thrust back against him. A deep, ragged groan escaped him as she rocked.

"You are so tight," he groaned, sinking deeper inside her, burning her alive. White hot heat scorched her flesh, singeing her nerves. She was so desperate for completion, she thought she would die from it.

His cock jerked inside her, responding to the agonizing clench of her rear muscles. Her womb convulsed, seizing as he sank to the hilt inside her and hoarse cries erupted from deep inside him. His seed burst into her, leaving her trembling, achy muscles shuddering as he pulled from her depths.

He fell onto the ground beside her, breathing heavily. He lay there long moments, quiet as she absorbed what happened.

"I begin to enjoy your pleasures, Alex. I fear what want of you does to my immortal soul," he finally whispered. Before she had a chance to respond, he got to his knees and stood, dragging her up with him.

Saying nothing more, he got onto his horse and helped her up, seating her before him. Alex resisted the impulse to cry out as her bottom connected with the hard saddle. Her cleft felt raw with need, her rear hole bruised from his loving. She'd enjoyed the feel of him inside her, but it couldn't mask the hurts. Were she on foot, it would not bother her, but the horse's bouncing as he trotted was agony on her sore bottom. She wiggled, trying to get comfortable. Just as she'd nearly succeeded, he scowled. "We will never make it home if you do not cease your squirming against my groin."

She moved again, eliciting another groan from him. "I am sorry, but I cannot help it. My ... buttocks ache," she said, trying to hold still.

He sighed heavily and pulled to a stop. She felt him move behind her, and then he said, "Stand in the stirrups while I slip this beneath you."

Bronson moved his feet, and she managed to stand enough that he slipped a cloth beneath her cheeks. When she sat down again, she was comforted by the feel of a cushion softening the harshness of the ride. Turning slightly, she saw that he'd removed his doublet.

Gooseflesh dimpled his flesh where it was exposed by his shirt and the slit of his tunic. His face was impassive, not showing a hint of softness. That he would suffer for her comfort infinitely warmed her. She faced ahead, smiling.

"My thanks," she murmured, snuggling back against his chest. He was warm despite his chill. Alex wanted to soak him into herself.

"You are welcome," he said gruffly, wrapping an arm around her midriff.

Her moment of peace lasted until they reached Derwin Hall, and then she realized how wrong she was to feel it.

Chapter Thirteen

"Have you received a response?" Hugh McPherson asked his runner.

"Nay, my lord, I've not."

"Damn," Hugh roared, slamming his fist on the table. The gathering of his kin looked at him in alarm.

"What is it, father?" Kiara asked with concern.

"That devil Blackmore refuses my missives and refuses to give the girl back to us."

"Do you wish to take her by force? Storm the castle?"

Hugh stroked the braids of his beard, eyeing his daughter shrewdly. "Nay, I don' wish it ta come ta that. Ne'er has there been bloodshed between us, I would not be the first to begin it."

"Then what?" Wren asked, perching atop a trestle as he took a sip of ale.

"I thought mayhap a few day's passing would

149

make him see reason, but I know now he will not. The gel has laid an enchantment on him, to be sure."

Kiara gave him a confused look. "I don't understand."

"If she ensnares him as I predict she will, he will do anything for her. She will ask to go to the market one day, or for a ride. When that time comes, we will spring upon him and take her back."

Murmurs of agreement rumbled through the room. "'Tis a good plan, indeed, father."

"Aye, I like it meself. Methinks she will not be long in wishing to free herself of that loathsome brood. After all, what McPherson could stand Blackmore company for any length of time, or vice versa." He chuckled at the thought, and sat back down, shooing the messenger away.

* * * *

Lord Derwin blustered down the front entranceway, scowling as Bronson and Alex rode up. "A fine son you are, Bronson. You set the house in an uproar when you tore out of here on that beast you call a horse. Constance has near worried me into an apoplexy with her concern over Lord Montague. What is all this commotion?" he asked, his face blooming with splotchy red patches.

Bronson dropped to the ground, helping Alex to her feet. "Alex esc—"

"I went for a stroll, your lordship," she interrupted Bronson, smiling at his father. "My apologies. I knew not how it would upset your household to find me gone."

150

Lord Derwin looked as though he might not believe her, but his complexion lightened and he smiled, clapping her on the back. "I'm glad you are returned. Mayhap we can go on a hunt today. Long has it been since I wandered these woods. Aye, I believe we will." He looked at the stablehand leading Ebony away. "You there, prepare mine and my sons horses, and young Alex's as well. We go for a hunt."

"It sounds a good adventure," Alex said weakly. Her knees shook, and she clutched Bronson for support.

"Father, I do not think Alex is ready to go off just now. His walk was overlong."

Lord Derwin glanced from Bronson's supportive hand to his face and back to Alex. He laughed suddenly. "Whyever not? Did you punish the boy for running off as he did?"

"Of a sorts," Bronson said quietly, shifting on his feet with discomfort.

Alex couldn't look at him. She was too afraid her guilt would show to Lord Derwin if she dared look up at Bronson's face.

Lord Derwin stroked his chin. "You go inside and break your fast. You'll see, it will improve the health of your flesh, and the hunt shall improve your spirits. You think I do not notice such things, but I've noticed a lagging in your energy these past few days, young Alex."

"Aye, my lord, it is so. I will join you in but a little," she said as she pulled free from Bronson and hobbled inside.

"I look forward to it!" he called after her, walking away to talk with Bronson.

Alex didn't care if they were even talking of her—all she wanted was to creep inside and collapse in her own bed. And she would, too.

No one disturbed her as she mounted the stairs and found her room. She locked the door behind her and dropped into bed, falling instantly asleep.

She awoke sometime later from a heated dream, unaware of how much time had passed. Regardless of her disorientation, she felt rested, but also disturbed by the dreams she'd been having. Bronson invaded even her sleeping thoughts. She could get no rest from him, nor did she know how much longer she could resist his sensual invasions, even in slumber. Her resistance seemed worn down to but a nub—nothing with which to shield herself from his potency.

Her womb ached, and as she shifted in bed, she realized she was wet with arousal, and still sticky from Bronson's earlier loving. Staggering from the bed, she poked her head out of the door and caught a passing servant, summoning them to prepare a bath. She stumbled back to bed as she waited a goodly while until they began filing in, hauling in the large basin for bathing as well as linens and buckets of steaming water.

Their movement reminded her nothing so much as ants, and she dozed between their trips, nearly falling back into a deep sleep as images of soft, masculine lips teased the fringes of her mind. The shutting of the door roused her into full consciousness, and she stumbled out of bed, locking it firmly. Alex stripped her dusty clothing off, removing her grass stained hose, tunic, and doublet, until all that remained was her shirt and the binding beneath it. The tub awaited her, but steam roiled off the hot water, and dragging a hand through the calm surface near burned her fingers and turned them red with the heat.

Feeling inexplicably lazy, she opted to doze a little while longer rather than risk scorching her hide, and she crawled back into bed. The moment she closed her eyes, fantasies of Bronson assaulted her, as if her mind was reluctant to give up the dream that tormented her.

He stood with his back to the fire, facing the bed, his chest rising and falling with each deep breath. Naked and wet, his skin glistened in the flickering light of the fire. His eyes were drowsy with lust, brazenly raking up and down her naked flesh, settling on the pink lips between her thighs with a look of possession.

She longed to wrap her arms around him, feel the play of muscles in his back, stroke her legs down his own.

As if she'd called him, he was suddenly on the bed, moving between her parted knees, watching her face contort with ecstasy as he rubbed a hand on her intimate parts. Some sound pierced her dream—her own consciousness seeking to destroy the rapture—dissipating the sweet feel of his fingers toying with her folds.

Alex moaned with frustration, stretching a hand to her apex, cupping herself as the dream ebbed. She was wet with longing, her cleft quivering with

153

unfulfilled desire. Her fingers slipped in the thick cream surrounding the hard bud. It seemed to jump as she rubbed across it, and she gasped at the exquisite pleasure that mounted. Her drowsiness waning, she sat higher in bed, spreading her thighs wide as she stroked the bud. Blood swelled it, heightening sensation until she panted for breath.

The feeling Bronson had closed in on her before neared, that same building of sensation that was so evocative with mystery. Her core clenched with longing and emptiness. What would happen if she had something inside her?

Alex sat higher, at an angle, parting her thighs as wide as they would go as she moved her other hand down and pushed through her folds and edged the entrance to her vagina.

Just slipping near the spot had her back arching, it felt so wondrous. She increased the rubbing slide on her bud, pushing a forefinger inside her passage. Pleasure bloomed on her nerves, heat uncurling deep in her belly, sliding excitingly through her being.

She withdrew her finger, mimicking the motion of Bronson's shaft in her rear hole, imaging his cock filling her sheath. She gasped as the bliss soared and came crashing through her. She cried out, rubbing her bud frantically, pushing inside herself harder, as deep as she could reach but not nearly deep enough. He would be larger than her finger, agony and ecstasy that she would welcome. The bed shook with her movement, mattresses groaning as she fought for release. Sweat blossomed on her flesh as she moaned, following the path of ultimate pleasure. Tremulous waves erupted suddenly, quivering through her sex.

She collapsed, dropping her hands to her sides weakly, her insides twitching with receding pleasure.

* * * *

Bronson was worried when Alex didn't come down for the hunt. He thought of going to her door, but knew if she slept, he would disturb her. It was also possible if she was awake, she would likely ignore him, and he would be no better off with knowing if she was well or not.

The weakness she'd displayed upon their arrival disturbed him. He was in agony, thinking he'd hurt her somehow, but thinking back on their joining, he could not remember signs that she'd suffered a hurt. He hadn't had adequate lubrication, of course, and the saliva he'd rubbed on his shaft was minimal. It was possible she'd sustained injury. With that thought, he felt like tearing off and storming upstairs to check on her, but he dared not until he'd occupied his father with other matters.

Once he'd gotten father to delay the hunt until after luncheon, he went inside and ducked into the elaborate servant's passages that traveled the length of the castle. Nearly every room had alternate access to it, as well as hidden spy holes known only to members of the family. He hadn't mentioned it to Alex when she'd appropriated the key to her room from him—he'd always known he had other ways of going inside should it be necessary. And, of course, the spy holes could prevent her from ever knowing he could see her. They'd been used in times past for various intrigues, and with King Henry, and under his father's rule, the Blackmore generations had had to use every means at their disposal to survive the volatile times.

He was glad he'd thought to put it to use now, so that he could see about her. He felt certain she slept, but he could not contain the concern that bid him see for himself.

Bronson raced up the dangerously narrow stairs, taking no heed to his safety. The passages were shallow, strung with dusty cobwebs that clung to his shoulders as he passed through them. He brushed them off, forging ahead until he was certain he neared her room. Heat suffused him, radiating from the wall, soaking through the stonework from the fireplace inside, and he knew he'd come upon the entrance that led into Alex's chamber. He unplugged the small eye holes, freezing in place at the sound that drifted to his ears. Moans of pain sent alarm shafting through his gut, making his heart clench painfully.

He peered through the eye holes, his alarm instantly changing to pure lust. Alex sat on the bed, her legs splayed wide, her fingers buried in her folds.

His cock roared to life, straining against his cod piece, demanding freedom. Bronson clenched his jaw on the pain, knowing he should look away from her, but unable to stop. The image of her, her mouth open on a moan, her eyes closed with desire, tortured him abominably. Her arm moved in a tremulous motion, slowly gaining in confidence as she found the right stroke to bring her ultimate pleasure.

His blood pumped furiously, pounding hard in his groin, feeling as though it would beat him to death. Stifling a groan, Bronson unleashed it. His engorged length sprang into his palm, and he wrapped his hand about it, stroking himself as he watched her, imagining the feel of her silken glove wrapped about him. He bit his lip, pressing his face against the wall as if it would get him closer to her.

He pumped his cock, his curled hand slipping up the rim surrounding its head, increasing the acute pain drawing through his veins. He watched as she thrust a finger inside herself, arching against it, widening her thighs, her fingers moving frantically now. He felt her frenetic need even at the distance, a mirror to his own longing.

Frenzy stormed him. He stroked himself harder and faster, bruising his flesh. His throat ached as he restrained his moans of passion, the desperate longing to bury inside her unbelievable now. She jerked against her fingers, crying out, sending him over the edge. His cocked throbbed, seed erupting from its tip to spew on the wall before him. He continued to pump until the life drained from him and his shaft grew flaccid in his palm.

Shuddering, muscles jerking with tension, he enclosed his aching flesh back in his cod piece and watched as she weakly moved from the bed and into a waiting tub. Mists of steam rose as she broke the water's surface.

She was so close to him now. If he took but two steps, he would be upon her. She leaned her head back on the tub's edge, closing her eyes, rubbing her hands up and down her arms, across her chest before resting them on the edge as well.

Already life stirred in his groin to see her laying there, vulnerable, near naked and wet. She would be slick, ready for his cock even as he readied for her. His own hand was no appeasement for his appetites—never had it been, and never would it satisfy, not as long as she lived. There was but one way to satisfy his desire, and by God, he would satiate his taste for the woman. Now.

For too long she had tormented him, for eons it seemed, beguiled him with her mystery. He would know the taste of her woman's flesh, the feel of her breasts in his palms, the sight of her hair unbound.

Bronson unlocked the door, easing it open. She did not stir as he passed into the room and closed the door gently behind him. She appeared to almost be asleep, her toying having sated her to exhaustion.

Bronson was in no way satisfied. Without sound, he strode to the tub, standing over her, willing her to open her eyes and look up at him. Slowly, she did, her eyes widening with horror.

She shrieked and covered her chest, sloshing water over the sides of the tub. "How did you get in here?" she demanded, looking frantically back at the door.

"I have my ways," he said gruffly, heat suffusing him at the wild look in her eyes, the soft parting of her lips. His cock swelled, his cod piece growing unbearably tight. Throwing away caution and care, Bronson bent and grasped her shirt, ripping the neckline open to her navel.

Alex screamed and ducked down into the water.

Bronson caught her arms, hauling her up until he could lay eyes on the binding across her breasts. "What is this?" he demanded, giving her a hard look, wondering if she would divulge her secrets now that she'd been exposed. He'd gone beyond the point of caring if she did or not. He knew she would never trust him, for he did not deserve her trust, in any form.

Alex gaped, clawing at his arms for release. "A wound, nothing more, my lord," she gasped, her feet slipping in the tub as she fought for purchase.

"I would see this wound," he said low, pulling her to her feet. "Strip the binding, Alex. I want to know that you've not come to great harm in my household."

Alex straightened her shoulders, the fingers of one hand going to the binding. She looked at him a long moment, as if stunned at her predicament. He recognized the look in her eye, knew just before she moved that she would bolt. She whirled around, running, her soaked feet slipping on the wet floor.

Bronson caught her before she could fall and do herself injury, propelling them both onto the bed. She yelled as he came down on her, bucking, scrabbling for freedom on her backside and elbows. She glared up at him, the fire in her eyes burning him alive. His groin felt near to bursting having her beneath him, struggling against desire.

Bronson straddled her waist, pinning her elbows down with his knees. She cursed him, panting and collapsing back as she realized the futility of her continued fighting. Her eyes widened as he withdrew a slim dagger from a sheath at his waist, angling it toward the binding on her chest. She jerked involuntarily as he sliced the linen away, working through the layers until he could reasonably grasp the edges and not worry on hurting her.

Slipping the dagger back in place, he took hold of each cut edge and pulled, ripping the binding and freeing her breasts. Alex gasped in outrage, struggling, her breasts bouncing free of their confinement. Bronson watched them in a daze, his salivary glands tightening. Her small breasts plumped up like soft rounded pillows, the pale flesh red from her constriction, her blushing pink nipples engorged and standing at attention.

Bronson swallowed, struggling through the lust laden cloud fogging his gaze. His voice hoarse from want, he said, "What is this, Alex? I see no wound here, but find woman's flesh instead. Do mine eyes deceive me?"

She was watching him steadily when he chanced to look back on her face. Her eyes were wide with fright and something else, and she seemed to hold her breath with expectation. She sucked at her bottom lip as though trying to work moisture into her mouth, but she did not speak, did not dare try to stop him.

God help him, he could not turn back now.

"Have you deceived me all this time, or am I struck with accursed vision for my sins of the flesh?" he asked hoarsely, unable to tear his eyes away from hers as he slid off her waist and backed down her hips. She held still, waiting to see what he would do.

"I am damned, for I cannot help but doubt. I wouldst have more proof, if err mine eyes," he growled, shifting down her thighs onto the bed, grasping her knees as he forced her legs to part.

Chapter Fourteen

Fear unlike any she'd ever known before froze Alex to the bed. She could not breathe. She could not think. All she could do was watch as Bronson stripped the soaked binding and exposed her breasts to his view, looking at her chest as though he wished nothing more than to eat her alive. A stillness possessed him a long moment, winding the tension within her, and then he was speaking again, moving.

When he moved down her legs and parted her thighs with rough hands, his fingers slipping on her still wet flesh, exposing her intimate folds to his vision, she thought she would die from the ecstatic pulse of desire that seized her insides at the hot rake of his gaze on her woman's flesh.

Alex bit her lip to keep from crying out as he held her gaze, dipping his head between her thighs. Her belly jerked on an anticipatory spasm.

Hot breath scorched her flesh, and then his tongue pierced her wet, swollen folds, moving straight to the nub that had so longed for his touch. Alex's hips jumped off the bed as he stabbed her with the molten tip, flicking it across her to capture the cream lading her nub.

"It seems you are indeed a woman," he growled into her slit before swathing his tongue down through the heavy honey that saturated her.

Alex gripped the sheets, her skin frigid and wet, but heat suffusing her from the inside out. "Nay, my lord. You cannot!" she breathed, her thighs trembling as he pushed them as far apart as they would go. His hands curled around her buttocks, cupping her as though she were a vessel of ambrosia and his for the taking.

He nuzzled her pubic mound with his nose, fanning his breath across her folds. "I can and will," he said, his voice rough, thick with lust. "My thirst is great, Alex. I fear only your honeyed sweetness can slake it.

The rough possessive timbre of his voice resonated low in her belly. Alex shook her head, closing her eyes, unable to look at his dark head nestled between her thighs. The sight of him there overcame her, heightening the lust that embraced her, saturating her femininity until she thought it would draw all the moisture from her body.

Bronson tilted her hips up to his lips. She felt the soft brush of his lips on her folds, heard his intake of breath as he inhaled her scent. He held her still when she would squirm, allowing her to know he was in absolute control.

"Look at me, Alex," he ordered, and she obeyed.

Dark were his eyes, smoldering as though a fire had been lit. He'd seen her secret and still he wanted her, wanted more. A sharp, desperate spasm of lust arched her insides at his dark look. She wanted to close her thighs, protect herself from the heat of his gaze, the molten swipe of his tongue. He was too much, too intense for her to survive. Looking on him made her womb tremble, that bud throb responding with achy tension.

"Know that you can hide nothing from me, Alex. Not this, not anything. You are mine," he said, his voice rough, deeper than she'd ever before heard it. It vibrated inside her, echoing in the desire gripping her body.

Before she could prepare, before she could take a breath to utter his name and deny his possession, he dipped his head and plunged his tongue deep in her core. Alex screamed, throwing her head back and grinding her hips up to his face, her sheath gripping his tongue as he curled it inside her, lunging forward, retreating.

His fingers dug into her buttocks, bringing her closer to his face as he ate her flesh, drank the syrup of her body as if he were starving. He devoured her, plunging inside again and again, mimicking the stroke his cock had set inside her anus until she was mindless with the feel of his molten slide in and out of her.

He lapped her, nibbling her folds with his lips, her juices making wet sounds that should have embarrassed her, but his greed for her honey allowed none to escape, and allowed her no chance to think beyond the pleasure racing inside her veins. He burrowed deep inside her, grinding his chin against the narrow strip between her entrances, rubbing his nose against the swollen bud.

He would smother, would eat her alive. His breath was ragged against her, fanning the desire burgeoning through her core.

He pulled out suddenly, panting as if from exertion. Alex whimpered, opening her eyes to see him watching her.

Knelt between her splayed legs, he removed his tunic and shirt, leisurely drawing them over his head. Each inch of flesh exposed by his movement sent sharp shafts of desire coursing through her. His skin was naturally dark, almost bronze, the muscles of his stomach jerked with his heaving breath, making her own lungs labor for air.

He threw the garments down, dropping his arms to his sides, his hands clenching, so near his cod piece, she wanted to scream from the anticipation. He'd left her on the edge, and she would die if he did not plunge into her and quench the burn of her loins.

He backed off the bed, standing. Alex made a small, disappointed noise, sitting up on her elbows. His lips curled in a slow, wicked smile, barely traceable, the slightest change in his expression that told her he enjoyed her torment and would prolong it as long as he wished. Alex shifted on the bed, frowning as she chewed her bottom lip, drawing his eyes to her mouth.

His eyes narrowed, studying her, holding her

gaze as he untied the lacing holding his cod piece in place. His cock jutted forth, impossibly thick, angrily red and swollen. He bent, blocking her view of it as he removed his hose and boots, and then he stood before her, unadorned save for his own masculine beauty.

Her breath caught in her throat to look on him, to see his eyes blaze like the hottest fire, a sapphire flame that singed her flesh and burned away her reservations. His black hair clung damply to his face and neck, and she itched to run her fingers through it, to have the hair matting his chest caress her breasts and belly. And that steely rod … what would it feel like in her most intimate core, rending, ramming, leaving nothing untouched…?

"You devour me, sweet Alex," he growled softly, advancing on her, crawling onto the bed toward her. Sensual menace oozed from his pores, dripped from his voice. He advanced on her with the leisure of a hunter who'd cornered his prey. "I could find release merely from your eyes."

Alex swallowed, backing away, her heart fluttering in her chest like a caged animal. "Why do you not," she whispered, choked with some indefinable emotion. She couldn't help but to glance down at his shaft, protruding from his groin like a lance seeking a target.

He caught her line of sight and smiled with pure, male satisfaction, crawling between her raised knees. "I have. 'Twas not near enough to appease me. I watched as you plunged a finger into your sheath. Listened to your moans of pleasure. I vowed I would make you scream for my cock inside you, for my mouth at your breast, my fingers in your slit."

Alex shuddered, wanting to look away but not daring to close her eyes. "Oh God. You ... you saw me?" She blushed, her skin turning crimson with mortification.

"Aye. My hand was little appeasement compared to the beauty of your flesh. Drinking your cream but whet my appetite," he said, crawling over her, closing her in with his body. He leaned over her on his forearms, his hair hanging down, his eyes unblinking, consuming her.

He bent his elbows, sinking inexorably down until his mouth was inches from her own. Shifting his hips, he rubbed the molten tip of his erection against the top of her pubic mound, letting her feel the weight of him.

"Do you feel how hard I am for you?" he murmured, closing the distance between their mouths in a fiery kiss.

Alex whimpered as he ground his hips against her, up against that white hot center of pleasure that throbbed for want of him. His tongue thrust deep into her mouth, stealing her breath and the essence of her soul in a devouring kiss that threatened to consume her. She suckled his tongue, thrusting off the tattered remains of her soaked shirt from her arms so that she could feel the silk of his skin against her flesh.

He groaned as she wrapped her arms around him, touching his back, her questing fingers discovering he was more gloriously hard and powerful than she'd ever imagined. His muscles flexed with strength beneath her fingers, responding to her touch. His flanks heaved with breath against her arms as he tore from her mouth and dragged his lips across her jaw.

Alex gasped, scored by his teeth, scraped by fledgling beard, his whiskers burning and feeling heavenly rough on her skin.

He lifted suddenly, propping on one arm, laying half atop her as he peeled her mustache away and ripped the wig from her head. Alex startled, her eyes widening with surprise, stunned to see him frowning down at her with brows heavy over his eyes.

"I want you as the woman you are," he growled, thrusting a hand in her hair to loosen the tight mat it had become. The silky fine tresses sprung to life at his touch, wove through his fingers like wisps of flame.

She felt free, unbound, a wildness soared inside her. His eyes darkened, near black from the shadow of his hair, but no less potent. She shivered, meeting his gaze.

"Somehow, I knew my wildcat would have hair of fire," he whispered, clutching the side of her head as he kissed her once more.

His mouth was sweeter this time, as if he'd pulled the emotion choking her lungs and bathed her with honey. Alex's throat tightened, her eyes stinging as he pleasured her mouth, nibbling her lips, her tongue, fueling the bittersweet desire.

The soft side of him stunned her, made her ache in places that should never hurt. Her heart seemed to trip over itself, its pace climbing as he smoothed a trail of kisses down the column of her throat to her breasts. He nuzzled her breasts, dragging his lips over the tender flesh, swiping his tongue across each nipple in turn.

With his free hand, he cupped her, rolling her nipple between his fingers, stoking the blaze consuming her loins. Alex's whimper of pleasure turned to a cry as he closed his mouth on one bare peak, dragging her flesh into his mouth in a hard, sucking kiss, rubbing his tongue on the delicate nipple until it swelled and hardened in his mouth.

She dug her short nails in his back like talons, crying out as he continued to suckle as though drawing sustenance from her breast. Her back arched, unconsciously thrusting her breasts closer. His lips and teeth, his tongue, were torture, undeniably sweet agony.

"I shall go mad without surcease," she breathed, risking a hand to clutch his head to her breast. She wanted him to stop, but she couldn't bear it.

He broke from her flesh, scoring the underside of her breast with his teeth before moving for her other. "As you have driven me mad," he growled, latching on, sucking near to the point of pain.

Tears squeezed from her eyes. Her vagina clenched in agony. Moisture flooded her, soaking her folds, seeking to cool that branding iron that pressed against her mound that offered no relief.

Alex planted her feet flat on the bed, arching her back, shifting her hips to raise and grind herself on his manroot. His hardness touched her cream laden bud, increasing the swell of it, the pain that gripped her—but what glorious pain it was. His mouth stilled. His body went rigid. His breath suddenly panted from him, chest heaving against her ribs.

"By my troth—do not!" he said hoarsely, closing his eyes.

Sweat beaded on his forehead, his arms. Alex bit her lip, lowering her arms until she could reach his buttocks. She grasped them, pulling him against her as she arched her hips, seeking that wondrous place yet again, finding it with his heated rod.

He groaned, long and loud, a mournful sound that erupted from deep inside him. He eased back, breaking her grip, and then she felt the change come over him. His muscles shook with the power of restraint. A great, hard knob pushed against her woman's sheath, stretching, tearing her, setting her flesh on fire.

Alex whimpered, needing his length inside her, knowing that the pain was what she craved … and she would have it. She moved her hips, forcing him inside her, gasping as the broad head of his cock distended her opening, moving past the fragile entrance. Her muscles seized on him, closing down, desperate to shut him out.

"Oh God," he panted, burying his face against her neck, shuddering with the effort of control. "I cannot."

"Please," she pleaded, dying, pinned to the bed and unable to move as she wanted—needed. She would expire without him. She'd gone too far to stop now. The pain had built inside her until she was near to bursting.

She dug her fingers into his buttocks, urging him to take her. His breathing quickened. She could feel the pound of his heart against her chest.

"Do ... not ... move," he groaned harshly. He dropped on her, melding to her, propping his weight on his elbows on either side of her ribcage.

Alex could not obey him, not in this. Hurt noises whimpered from her throat. She rubbed her legs against his, her calves to his thighs, stimulating her senses, awakening sensation in her lower half. Her entire body seemed sensitized to the slightest touch. She moaned, breathing heavily, rubbing her legs, locking them around his buttocks as she stroked her palms up his back.

A loud, mournful cry tore from him. He bit her neck, stifling it, shaking, breathing hard and fast through his nose. His muscles flexed, tensed as if to hold him back, but he'd lost his mind, all control. He thrust, ramming the broad length of himself inside her, tearing, rending flesh. Alex screamed as he tore through her maidenhead and sank to the hilt in her sheath.

He shuddered, and she felt hot tears against her neck, knew not if they were his or her own. His cock twitched against her breached inner muscles. The breath had stolen from her lungs at the force of his invasion—she couldn't breathe for the weight of him, the wound he'd struck inside her.

Slowly, drawing out her agony, he pulled his

shaft from her core, rubbing that impossibly hard, huge knob through her tender insides until his cock was nearly free, and then he plunged deep once more.

Alex cried at his gentle push, clenching him, aching as he withdrew, aching as he entered. With each stroke, she thought surely now she would die, but slowly, as he continued subjecting her to the movement she'd craved so much before, tremors built inside her. The fire in her muscles ceased to burn with pain, searing instead with an increasing pleasure. It felt like his tongue but harder, more demanding. He was so huge, he filled her near to overflowing. He stretched her sheath so tightly, she could feel the engorged veins roughing his length, bumping through her muscles.

Her legs tightened involuntarily, hooking beneath his buttocks, urging him deeper, harder. Pleasure scored her, erupting along her nerves. Alex moaned as he increased his tempo, gliding through the arousal soaking her folds, searing her from the inside out.

He sucked her neck hard, branding her with his mouth. Alex arched against him, clawing his back, tilting her head deep in the pillows. The bed shook with his movement, quaking around them, echoing their groans of pleasure and pain.

Pleasure mounted, amplifying from its fragile beginnings into a force that threatened to explode within her, destroy her sanity if she could not reach it.

He blistered her with his molten rod, stroking, ramming, grinding against the swollen bud with each push until all her senses focused on the one place, screaming for release. Her blood boiled. Her flesh scalded with his touch.

It overwhelmed her, erupted through her muscles, dissolving flesh and bone. Alex screamed, jerking against him as the orgasm rippled through her in a wave that melted her, molded her to his body. She clung to him, desperate to hold on to the pleasure, tightening her hold until she could no longer feel her arms or legs—only the ecstasy, swirling inside her. He groaned, arching his back, throwing his head back as he raised on his arms, thrusting into again, his movements disjointed, hurried. His cock throbbed inside her, seed erupting from its tip deep in her womb.

He collapsed on her, crushing her, but she did not mind. Their heavy breath mingled, their sweaty bodies clung to one another.

Slowly, sight and sound returned as the bliss ebbed. Bronson rolled, dragging his flaccid cock free of her body with a loud smack, pulling her on top of him to cuddle her on his chest. Her hair cascaded around them in a fine tangle, and he ran his hands through her tresses, dislodging the snarls with gentle thoroughness.

Alex lay there, enjoying the feel of his hands in her hair, the sound of his heart near her ear. Her body was sore and tired, close to exhaustion, but it was exhilarated as well, a contradiction that astounded her. She could not help the madness he'd slipped over her, coaxed her into with forceful gentleness.

Having him like this wounded her, for she knew it could not last. She'd lain there long enough, reveled overlong in the feel of his arms and the warmth of his body. Touching him dissolved the strength of her will, and she could not survive without it.

Alex lifted her head, looking up at him. His eyes were closed as he toyed with her hair. His brow was unmarred by worry, lighter, some of that darkness that had so terrified and beguiled her was diminished.

She pushed at his chest, intent on standing and washing herself in the cooling water, relieving herself of his scent on her skin.

He opened his eyes at her movement, giving her a dark, possessive look, aggression permeating the sudden tenseness of his muscles. With unmatched speed, he shifted his hands to her shoulders in a merciless grip.

Alex stiffened, grasping his forearms but not attempting to break his hold.

"I see the intent in your eyes," he ground out, shaking her when she tried to look away, forcing her to meet his gaze.. "I will not give you up, Alex. You are mine, always," he said, his voice tight and forceful.

Chapter Fifteen

Bronson angrily thrust away from her, sickened at his actions. She weakened his will, destroyed his resolve to stave himself from her. He glanced back where she lay on the bed, naked, her thighs smeared with blood and his seed, saw that her maidenhead stained the bedcovers and felt like heaving his guts out for his trespass. He was caught between disgust for taking what did not belong to him, and desire to steal it again, to go back to the bed and ram her depths, mold her to his cock until she screamed his name and he knew she would never scream another.

His cock hardened to see her as a woman, her fine hair tangled around her shoulders, curling around her breasts. He'd thought to assuage his hunger for her. Instead, he'd only increased his appetite.

Bronson turned away, striding to the tub. The

water was still warm. It seemed a lifetime had passed since he'd seen her touching herself, since he'd taken her innocence, but little time had, in truth, elapsed.

He stepped into the tub, enjoying the warmth that eased over his skin. He watched her across the room, gathering her hair onto the crown of her head, trying to shield herself from his gaze by turning her back to him.

"Come, the water is still warm, and you needs must bathe the ruin of your maidenhead from your thighs."

A small, hurt sound escaped her, but she stood and walked to him, eyes downcast, feet dragging. He felt her torn sound in his gut, felt it clench his heart. He angrily thrust it away, remembering who she was, what she'd done. He should not care if he hurt her—he would not care.

She stopped before him, turning her back to him to step into the tub. "Nay," he said, halting her. "I would have you face me. I want to watch you bathe."

A shiver ran visibly up her spine, but she turned, stepping into the tub. It was a small vessel, not near large enough for two people. She was forced to sit on his extended legs, her knees on each side of him. Gooseflesh dimpled her skin as she dipped a cloth in the water and ran it up her arms, across her chest. Her hair trailed in the water, clinging to her skin in places, and floating on the surface in others.

He watched her slip the cloth over her breasts, darting a glance to her face, saw her bite her lip as if pained. His cock throbbed to life, standing from his belly.

He could not bear it, to watch her but not touch. With a hoarse groan, he reached across the short distance and wrapped his hands around the small of her back, hauling her against him. He startled a gasp from her, her eyes shot daggers at him, but her lids dipped with lust. Her thighs slipped around his hips and he gripped her cheeks, spreading her as wide as he could as he lifted her and impaled her on his staff.

She cried out, arching her head back, gripping his shoulders, her sheath tight on his cock. He pumped up, into her, groaning, grunting at the vice of her body, the pain she inflicted on him with her sex.

He kissed the front of her arched neck, holding her closer, tightening his strokes. It was easier now, the pleasure before ripe for the plucking. Her womb trembled around him, she panted, gasped, bloodied his back as her orgasm quivered inside. The rhythmic convulsion of her muscles was his undoing. He came inside her, thrusting until he was certain she must tear above the pounding of his cock. Silk gripped his cockhead, sucking the seed from his body.

He groaned against her neck, gasping, breathing raggedly as the mind numbing pleasure roared through his veins and out through his cock. He rammed inside her until there was nothing left, until she'd taken every measure he had to give, and still, he wanted her to have more.

Never, never could he have enough of her. The thought rent his mind, turning him to madness.

* * * *

Bronson held Alex captive in the bed the remainder of the day. His father's hunt was delayed until the morrow—he'd seen to that after he'd had the bath taken away and she'd hid beneath new, unstained covers he'd pulled from the chest. She hadn't dared try to bar the door against him while he was gone, for he was in a mood that allowed no resistance, and God save her, she was of little mind to fight him.

Let her have this one day of ecstasy—it would end soon enough. He could not keep her locked away forever.

He brought a platter of food for them when he returned, as well as wine. He fed her the choicest morsels, pampered her, brushed her hair and soothed the aches of her body with his hands. With the aches of her femininity, he soothed with his lips and tongue, delving deep to the twinges of pain in her core, until he drove her to arch against him in mindless wanting.

She felt bruised from his loving, and each touch brought pleasure crashing down around her. Finally, she fell asleep in his arms to the feel of him brushing her hair back from her forehead and kisses upon her temples.

She awoke an indeterminate time later to his lips on her cheeks and jaw, his hands on her back, cupping her against his hardness. She moaned, responding already, her sex awash with arousal. He coaxed a thigh around his hip, urging her to touch him. She stretched her arm between their bodies, gripping his engorged staff, fascinated by its silky strength and heat. She loved the soft groan in his throat as she brushed her thumb over the tip, wondered at the tensing of his muscles, the movement of his throat as he swallowed hard on the passion.

She lifted her thigh, and he squeezed the cheek of it, cuddling her closer as she guided his cock into her tight entrance. Pain ebbed along her nerves, but it was good, so delicious as he slid deep inside her. She rubbed her bud, slipping in her creamy arousal, smearing it on his cock to ease his passage.

He moaned, kissing her forehead, thrusting his hips against her, trapping her hand to her bud. She rubbed it, clenching on his cock, gasping as he plunged with short, vivid strokes in her depths.

He made slow, gentle love to her, gliding through her wetness. Her sheath seemed formed for him already, and she was unable to imagine anyone else ever touching her so deeply.

Bliss crashed from the frantic move of her fingers, the pulse of him in her depths. She moaned, freeing her hand to clutch his arm and widen, take him deeper. He sank as far as the position allowed, spewing seed inside her, giving her achy release and then holding her to the feel of him as he drained his life into her womb.

He gave her no time to wonder at his possession, no time to worry on the future. There was only now—this.

She wanted to question his motives, but each time she opened her mouth to speak, his kissed her and stole the words from her mouth, sucked

179

the speech from her tongue.

Exhausted, sated, they slept through the night.

When the sun broke through the darkness, Alex knew the wonder she found in his arms was lost to her.

* * * *

Bleary-eyed, Alex stared at Bronson's back with a mixture of irritation and a curious sort of admiration. She would not have been particularly thrilled at the idea of being dragged out on a hunt at any time. After the night she had just spent in Bronson's arms, straddling a horse was the last thing she had any interest in doing.

There was no part of her privates that didn't throb with a combination of fond reminiscence and pure unremitting pain. Realizing some of it was caused in part by the heavy, oaken leg laying across her thighs and the meaty arm around her waist, she sighed, easing herself out from under him.

Her slow, cautious movements alerted him. He shifted until he'd turned his head toward her. A familiar light gleamed in his eyes, and his hand tightened at her waist. "Where do you go, wild-cat?"

She stilled, tamping down the beat of her heart. "'Tis the morn. My belly is empty and craves sustenance."

He pulled her closer, arching a brow. "I have just the thing to fill your insides."

"Nay," she cried, half laughing, half shrieking in horror. She planted her palms on his chest, holding him at bay. He would have none of it.

He dragged her to his length, holding her to him with leg and arm, kissing her breathless.

Her stomach growled.

Bronson broke from her mouth with a chuckle. "It seems I'm remiss in my duties," he murmured.

Alex flushed with embarrassment, ducking her head as he tried to kiss her again. He growled softly as he connected with her cheek. "Do you not remember what day this is? Have not you promised your father the hunt?" She regretted reminding him, but truthfully, now that she thought on it, she could at least handle her horse. There was no controlling the wild, bucking beast that was Bronson.

He sighed, rolling off of her. "You are right. I will leave you to dress," he said, slipping his hose and cod piece on as he gathered the remainder of his garments. "They will be breaking their fast by now. You'd do well to hurry if you want to quiet your belly's gnawing."

Alex scowled at him, clutching her stomach to muffle its noise. He ducked out, leaving her alone with her thoughts. She would find it hard to maintain her guise of young lord before the others. Bronson had not spoken a word of it, but for her own comfort, she must try.

Alex washed her face in the basin and wiped the residue from her thighs and folds with a damp cloth before donning her wig and mustache once more. Her hair seemed to have grown exponentially during the night, and she struggled to wind it tight enough to fit 'neath the wig.

Bronson had destroyed her binding, so she

wore her long tunic and a thick, padded jerkin, hoping the decorative slashing and padding would disguise her chest. Truth be told, she did not have much to hide, and with her cape on, hooked under one arm and across her chest, there was no telling she was any different from before.

Save for inside.

Alex shook it off, determined to go on as she had before and ignore soft feelings for Bronson. Frowning, she left and wandered down the stairs to the dining hall. Only the family remained inside at the late hour, obviously eager to begin their hunt, but lingering until the hunting party had gathered.

Lord Derwin laughed and clapped Bronson on the back, giving Alex a glance as she came inside and sat to eat.

"Glad to see you yet live, boy. I'd worried, it's been so many hours since last I saw you," Lord Derwin said, grinning as he turned back to Bronson. "I thought mayhap we'd travel the Northern wood. The bucks will be traveling with the weather, and I thought perhaps we'd bag one as a prize for your betrothed this day. Mayhap some ermine—their coats should soon be turned for winter."

Alex sucked in a sharp breath. Blood roared in her ears, drowning out the voices around her. She felt dizzy, as though she would faint. She gripped the arms of her chair, willing Bronson to lift his head and meet her eyes, to tell her it was a lie, a farce.

Bronson looked up at her sound of surprise,

his face hard, angry. His jaw clenched, his eyes darkened. She saw the truth there, in his rigid pose and silence.

Something tore inside her, bled, leaving her cold and lifeless, yet still she lived. Somehow, in the back of her mind, she'd hoped for a future with him—she realized that now, knew she'd denied her tender feelings almost to the point of blindness. All for naught! He was to marry another. He'd taken her innocence, claimed her as his own, possessed her soul with the fire of madness, the fury of passion. Never would he truly be hers.

He'd betrayed her.

He cast his eyes down, unable to face her. He stood up from the table suddenly, shoving his chair back, angrily striding away and slamming out of the hall.

"I see Bronson is in one of his terrors today," Gray said as he came in, rubbing his arm as if he'd struck something and injured it. No doubt Bronson had plowed through him on his way out. "Are we ready to ride, then?"

"Aye," Alex said, standing on weakened knees. "I'm ready to be gone." She'd lost her appetite. Her tongue felt wooden in her mouth. Her belly clenched in a miserable knot.

It had come to this, as she'd known it would. She was sick with it. She wanted free of this household, and she meant to escape this day. There would be no stopping her, even if she had to kill someone.

The horses were saddled and ready for their departure. Bronson took the lead with his father, leaving Alex to ride alongside Gray as Rafael took up the rear. Her rapier had been returned to her, and she'd been given a short bow and quiver.

Lord Derwin enjoyed the challenge of finding his quarry and giving chase without aid of hounds, nor did he make use of the common practice of frightening the wild creatures out of their burrows and homes with use of bells and men clacking sticks. The effect was pure adventure. She was against killing for sport, but she could not help the thrill of excitement that infected her as they urged their horses through the woods and caught sight of their first buck.

She enjoyed the freedom of the run, and for once, Firedancer was behaving himself, no doubt chagrined from spending over a week confined to the stables and little else.

Lord Derwin took aim but missed, laughing as he kicked his heels into his horse's flanks and gave chase. Alex thought him a madman for his strangeness, and wondered how any Blackmore had ever caught any living creature.

Gray and Rafael moved to the sides, intent on cornering it, and Bronson moved ahead.

Alex's heart stilled, realizing she'd been forgotten. She dwindled behind them, watching as they drew further and further ahead, racing through the forest of falling leaves and dead brush.

Knowing it was her one chance, Alex turned Firedancer, crashing through the tangling underbrush, heading North to Scotland as they went Westward deeper into the wood.

Chapter Sixteen

Bronson couldn't see Alex. Alarm knocked the breath from his lungs. He pulled hard on Ebony's reigns, turning around, letting his father and brothers outrun them as they vaulted after the buck.

She was gone. There was no trace of her in the forest. He saw nothing of her retreat, nor could he hear the sound of movement other than his own heart in his ears.

He knew where she'd gone.

His vision turned red. A murderous haze overtook him. She had left him. He didn't care if it was right, that he had no reason to expect her to stay. He still would not allow it—he could not allow it. Bronson kicked his horse into action, racing through the woods North.

He would find her. He refused to believe he would not.

The sounds of the hunt receded as he gained distance, ignoring the branches that slashed at him, the brambles that tore his hose at his passing. Ebony snorted, huffing as she ran, steadfast to his course.

The edge of the wood neared, until he could see green pasture beyond.

A cape fluttering caught his eye, red as a banner. He nudged Ebony forward, bursting from the wood, urging her faster, patting her neck, whispering words of encouragement as he lay low against her neck.

Alex heard him, kicked her heels against her horse, spurring him on. The heavy beast was no match for Ebony's grace and speed. She lunged forward, nearing his rearing, pulling forward, running neck and neck.

Bronson reached across the short distance, catching Alex's reigns. She slapped at his hand, but was too unsure of her seat to try more to ward him off, and their pace was too dangerous to take chances. Her horse tossed his head, snorting as Bronson eased them down, slowing their speed by finite degrees. He pulled hard on the reigns, halting them, lunging for Alex's wrist before she could twist away. He caught her arm, dragging her, kicking and screaming, off her horse and onto his lap.

She arched her back, trying to drop off his lap, losing her wig in her struggles until her hair fell down and tangled around them. She screamed in frustration as he held her arms tight, locking his knees against Ebony to keep from sliding off at her struggles.

She was breathing heavily from exertion, her face pink with her fury, her eyes wild and hair untamed. "Release me!" she screamed in impotent fury, squirming in his hold.

"Damn you," he growled, crushing her to his chest as he kissed her. She bit his lip, drawing blood. He grunted in pain, pulling back immediately, glaring at her.

"Do not touch me!" she railed in a furious whisper, as if suddenly fearful of alerting the others to his aid.

Bronson wiped the trickle of blood from his mouth, surprised to find she'd only scratched him with her canines. Already it stopped.

She gnashed her teeth at him, every inch the wildcat. No matter his fury, her anger, he wanted her still. His cock swelled with his rage, burned with the need to conquer. He gritted his teeth, the muscles in his jaw working.

"No, you are mine, damn you!" he said with quiet anger, giving her a shake to make her meet his eyes.

She met his gaze, letting him feel the wrath in her eyes. "You have no right! Go to your betrothed, find warmth and comfort in her arms," she said, choking, her voice breaking with emotion.

He was stunned to see tears in the corners of her eyes. His anger diminished to a low roar, and he bent to kiss her. "There is no other to satisfy as you do," he murmured.

"I hate you," she whispered, closing her eyes

in pain.

He covered her mouth, and her lips opened to him unwillingly. He felt the grooves of her teeth, asking for passage. Her tongue eased out, touched him, tremulously seeking.

He groaned and thrust his tongue inside, drinking the sweet wine of her mouth, enjoyed her small moans of pleasure. She shuddered against him, and he tightened an arm around her, resting one hand on her lap, guiding it under her tunic.

He cupped her sex, felt her moisture there, the wetness soaking his fingers. Her perfume released with the movement, tantalizing his nostrils with her faint fragrance. Groaning with desire, he mated with her tongue, thrusting his fingers against her sex, gratified to hear her moan in pleasure, move against his hand.

Distantly, through the fog of lust in his brain, he recognized the sound of riders approaching. He paid them no heed, not caring if they saw him kissing Alex or fondling her. Damn them if they tried to stop him.

His cock swelled against her bottom as she wiggled closer, kissing him harder, her soft lips pliant beneath his own. She placed a hand on his biceps, kneading the muscle as he curled his fingers into her sex.

"Unhand my niece before I strike you dead 'pon your horse."

* * * *

Chills raced up her spine at the threat. Alex broke from Bronson's mouth and saw, to her horror, that they were surrounded. Bronson tightened his hold on her, turning his horse so that he could face the threat.

"I'll not give her up without a fight," he growled, easing her to the ground as he reached for his sword.

One of the men had his blade out in an instant, the tip pressed against Bronson's throat. Bronson froze, glaring at the elder man he faced.

"My brothers will be here soon enough. You'll not get far, Hugh."

Hugh laughed, stroking his beard, chancing a glance at Alex. "I should run you through for the trouble you've caused."

"Nay," Alex screamed, standing before him. She could not stand by and watch as he was butchered. Surely these men, her cousins, could not be so heartless.

Hugh gave her a pitying look, returning his attention to Bronson.. His voice dropped and his look grew stormy. "No doubt you've stolen her maidenhead."

"It is no concern of yours," Bronson grit out, clenching and unclenching his hands.

"It is every McPherson's concern. Were you another man, I'd take you before the priest and force you to marry the gel. As it is, I'm afraid it's out of my hands. Come now, gel, get in yer saddle. We're off to home."

Alex looked at him, wanting to trust him. This was what she'd fought to do for so long. Now that it was upon her, she was reluctant to go. Not until she made certain no harm befell Bronson. "You will not hurt him if I come willingly?" she asked, not daring to look at Bronson for fear she would break down and cry.

Hugh frowned. "Nay, lovely. He will come to no harm, were you willing or no. I give you my word," he said, crossing himself—, "on the lives of my children."

Satisfied of his word, she smiled and climbed atop Firedancer. Hugh led her away while the others took care of Bronson. She glanced back, only to assure herself, and found they'd hauled him off his horse and were binding him.

She turned back to Hugh, determined to ignore the scene behind her. Hugh smiled at her kindly, reminding her of her grandfather. She felt tears bleed into her eyes.

"Come, Alex, is the hurt so severe?" he asked, urging them to a trot.

"Nay. I weep for things that can never be … and for those I can never have again." She was silent for a time, noticing the others had joined them but hung back in a protective gesture, wary but allowing a measure of privacy.

"How did you know me?" she asked suddenly.

He chuckled, his eyes crinkling with mirth. "'Twas my brother, your Uncle Argyle that saw you on a raid. He told us you had the bonny look of Heather, despite your guise. 'Twas not until your King Henry's messenger arrived, however, that we learned your true identity. By my troth, he knows more of you, a stranger, than we, yer kin."

Fear turned her blood to ice. The king—he'd found her! "What was his message?" she asked, amazed the king hadn't come crashing down upon her before now. The hunted feeling from before came again, closing her throat, clutching her gut. Her aches and pains diminished in the dread assaulting her.

"I do not remember it to the letter. He only told me of his search for you, that you need to make haste to his court, for he has a special engagement awaiting yer arrival."

Saints above! She knew what that cryptic message meant. She was not ready to be a wife. She'd learned nothing of their ways, knew not how to run a household and perform other wifely duties. All she knew were carnal pleasures, she realized with a blush.

"I gather from yer expression, this isn't fair news?"

Alex choked down her embarrassment, fighting back heated remembrances. "Nay 'tis not."

"I hate to give you up when we've only just found you, lass. Ye must know, we won't force you ta leave."

"I thank you," she murmured, falling into a comfortable silence as they journeyed on to Scotland. It warmed her to have family again, someone to protect her, someone she could call her own. She knew her duty, however. She would prepare for travel at the McPherson household, and then she would go to the king, no matter the discourse of her mind.

* * * *

Hours passed before the Blackmores located Bronson. They found him bound and gagged, lying on the ground with his horse tied to a nearby tree.

He was livid.

As soon as his bonds were cut, he was on his feet, steaming with silent fury. "They've taken her. Those damned devil's have taken her!"

Their father exchanged a look with Gray and Rafael. Gray shrugged. Rafael just looked embarrassed and confused.

Constance, who'd come to help search, laid a tentative hand on his arm, calming him enough he could speak with reason. "Who Bronson?"

"Alex!" he said, running his hands through his hair, throwing his head back to yell up at the sky.

Constance's eyes widened. "Who has taken her?" she asked again, catching his chin, forcing him to meet her eyes.

He gave her a thunderous look, his nostrils flaring with his heaving breath. Slowly, a weariness settled on him, making his tense shoulders slump with weight. "Her cousins, the McPhersons."

"What is this she business, son?" Father demanded gruffly.

"Alex is a woman, Father," Constance explained. All turned stunned eyes on her. She didn't smile though she should have been amused at their naiveté.

"What?" Father roared, leaning weakly on his horse. Gray hugged is shoulder, looking ill himself.

"How did you know?" Bronson asked, surprise etched on his hard face.

"In the stables. I came to realize it afterwards,

how odd his behavior. I've known for several days now. I'm surprised neither Gray or Rafael discovered this as well."

"Damn. But ... damn," Rafael murmured, sitting on the ground, propping his hands on his knees.

"I don't see how this could have happened," Father mumbled, rubbing his eyes. "I was fond of the boy. He—she was a good lad. So honest. Why would she deceive us?"

"I aim to find out," Bronson vowed.

"How so?" Gray asked, Constance echoing his words.

"I mean to steal into the McPherson's lair and take her back.

Chapter Seventeen

Alex was amazed by the size of her newfound family. Uncle Hugh ushered her into the ancient castle and into the midst of them. The men were fair-haired and broad, as tall as the Blackmores, but as different in appearance as night and day. Uncle Argyle she had 'met' before, as she sat in a cow patty during the raid.

He grinned at her. "I don' bite, lass. C'mon, get you inside to the rest of us. They're eager to lay kisses on yer cheeks."

Alex chuckled, breathless as each cousin hugged her in turn. Argyle had never married, but Hugh seemed to have made up for the loss by having many, many children. Her eldest cousin, Callum had a wild look to him, and he was far more quiet than his rowdy brothers. Next came Flynn and Hunter, the twins. There was Jamie and Wren, and lastly, she met the only female of the bunch—Kiara. Kiara's hair was darker than her own, perfectly straight, but her build was the same as her own, and she looked more sister to her than distant relative.

"I'll get ye away from these brutes so you can rest, cousin. Ye've had a tryin' day, I'm sure," she said with a laugh, pulling Alex free from the hugging bustle.

Alex grinned, tripping along beside her, giddy and happy. Her troubles seemed faraway now, and she didn't want to worry herself over matters out of her control. For now, she planned to enjoy her family.

Kiara led her upstairs to her solar, collapsing on a chair and gesturing Alex toward one.

Kiara breathed a sigh. "Whew, 'twas a job gettin' away from that brood. Tell me, how like you the family?"

Alex grinned. "I think I shall like you all very much."

Kiara returned her smile, then abruptly grew serious. Her voice full of concern, she asked, "Did you come to harm at Derwin Hall? If it's so, I'll take my blade to the lot of them."

Alex sighed, rubbing a hand along her cheek and jaw. "Nay, 'twas not so bad I am mortally wounded."

"I saw you, you know. As that lout, Bronson bathed and forced you to watch. I came in and saved you. Remember the maid with the linens?" She gave a little laugh. "You looked terrified. Not that I blame you. 'Twas understandable."

She swallowed, vividly remembering the first time she'd seen him bathing. Her body flushed with heat. She patted her hot cheeks. "I was not forced to do anything I did not want to do."

Kiara gave her a look. "I know the ways of their men. I gave one my mark for his trespass."

Alex sat up straight in her chair, intrigued. "Oh?

195

Which one?"

Kiara waved her hand, looking disinterested. "The one who's name is akin to mud."

Alex laughed. "Gray?" she asked, astounded. She'd been certain a while there, he was going to beat her for attempting to seduce his brother. She could just imagine what her cousin had done to him. "What did you do?"

"'Tis of no importance." She grinned suddenly. "Marry, I warrant he does not forget me," she said with a laugh, wiping tears from her eyes before straightening her face. "You'd do well to learn to protect yerself from men. Clinker me if they don't seem an entirely different species. You mark my words, no matter what father says, when the time comes, you run from the marriage bed. I've seen too many an unhappy bride even amongst our own clansmen."

"Aye," Alex agreed, nodding.

"So God mend me, I do go on. I fear I set you in a spell with my glum words."

"Nay, I enjoy your talk."

"I see yer sad. Come, let's join the others and be merry. I warrant they've scattered by now. One or two should not be so overwhelming," she said with a grin, standing and offering her hand to Alex. "I am glad yer here, cousin. It can be lonesome being surrounded by so many clods."

* * * *

Bronson, Gray, and Rafael ignored the warnings of their father and Constance's pleading. Bronson had made up his mind, and it would not be changed. Gray and Rafael vowed to go if only to protect Bronson from irreversible folly.

They waited through the following day until

night fell. The moon cast almost no light in the pitch dark, and the stars shed more than the pale sliver peeping through wispy cloud cover.

It took hours to reach the McPherson castle, for they had to leave their horses behind when they neared and walk the remaining distance. Fires glowed on the ramparts as clansmen kept watch in the frigid night air.

The three men studied the guards, following the patterns of their watch. They'd been to the castle once, long ago when they were unruly children intent on playing pranks on their neighbors. Bronson knew their only chance was the entrance they'd taken then, but he feared that it had come to ruin in the intervening years. If the tree had been trimmed, there would be no gaining access, and they would be caught in the open with no chance to escape.

He didn't believe they would be killed, but if the Scotsmen caught him trying to take back their kin, he honestly couldn't fathom how they would react.

"You mean to take the old oak?" Gray asked, whispering.

Rafael punched him on the shoulder. "They cannot hear us at this distance, airling."

Gray scowled. "'Tis a good measure to take, no matter our distance."

"Hold you two," Bronson said. "Aye, I take the route by the tree. Unless they've boarded the window or a storm as felled its branches, we should be able to gain entrance."

Gray rubbed his chin, looking at the castle. They couldn't see the tree, for it was in the back, shielding the garden that had once grown there when the lady of the manor still lived. "'Twas

197

ancient at the time and we young boys. I've my doubts they'd let it stand so long."

"I warrant the old man kept it for sentimental reasons."

"What are we waiting for then," Rafael asked.

Bronson tensed, crouching on the small rise. "By the next pass of yonder guard, we go down the hill to that ridge. From there, round the back." He gave his brothers a look. "You'll have to keep up."

Gray snorted. "I can beat you in a race any day, old man."

"We shall see," Bronson said, readying himself. He had a prize to claim this night—Gray and Rafael had not the incentive he possessed.

The guard walked as he'd done every other time, rounding the ramparts and heading to the far side, turning his back toward them.

Bronson lunged forward, racing down the rise, jumping the ragged terrain at its bottom as he headed for the castle. Gray and Rafael trailed him by a hair, moving silently.

Within heartbeats, they hit the castle, hugging their bodies tight against it. Bronson breathed through his teeth, listening for sounds of alarm. None came to his ears, and he edged quickly along the wall, moving round to the back.

He breathed in relief to see the ancient oak, unaware he'd held his breath as he moved around the corner tower. He looked up toward the window. A skin scraped to paper thinness covered it, but he could see no light inside the hallway that lay there.

Bronson moved to the tree, getting a grip on the rough wood, finding a handhold to haul himself up. He grunted as the bark scraped the flesh off his knuckles, but ignored it as he climbed his way up the branches.

One thick limb stretched toward the window like an arm. Bronson stood, listening a moment to his brothers grunt as they climbed the great trunk, and then he placed a foot on the limb. It seemed steady enough.

He held his arms out for balance, trusting the branch with his weight. Slowly, he walked. As he crossed half the distance, however, the limb groaned loudly, and wood snapped.

Bronson froze instantly, sweat beading his lip as he waited to go crashing down. He glanced over his shoulder at his brothers, who waited at its edge. "I fear it will not survive many trips," he whispered. "You must stay here."

"Nay, we go with you," Gray whispered loudly.

"I do not trust that it would survive more than this trip and my return. I go alone. You two wait for me here. If I do not return, know that they've taken me prisoner."

Releasing his breath and stilling his lungs as though it would lighten him, he continued walking. His face grew hot, his muscles ached with tension, but in moments, the window was there, close enough he could touch it.

Gathering himself, he stepped from the limb, stretching until his foot met the window's ledge. He leaned forward, trusting the sole of his shoe not to slip, and he grasped the window, pulling himself across the short distance. He hugged the frame, catching his breath, willing his blood to calm.

Finally, calm enough he could continue, he bent and peeled the skin loose, working it open so that he could step inside. Darkness swallowed him as he dropped to the stone floor.

He was on the second story. From the hazy childhood memories, he remembered the family and guest rooms were on this level. Below lay the great hall and other points of gathering as well as rooms for servants. He had no way of knowing which room she'd been given.

upon him.

Bronson crept down the hall, stopping at the first door he came upon. Heart hammering, he eased it open, discovering the room was empty. He breathed a sigh, part relieved, part frustrated. He moved on, checking each door. It seemed this wing was empty of anyone, for he found not a sign of life. These had to be the guest quarters, which comforted him somewhat. Surely she would have been sequestered here.

He was drawing near the main hall, evidenced by the spread of its passage and the torch lights illuminating it. He had but one more door to check. Steeling himself for disappointment, Bronson eased the door open.

Eyes adjusted to the dimness, he peered inside toward the bed at the back wall. Pale light streamed through a crack at the animal skin covering the window, casting just enough light with which to see the bed.

His heart stopped as he saw that it was occupied. He stepped inside, willing the raging blood to cease roaring in his ears. He crossed the room, making nary a sound, not stopping until he stood beside it and could gaze through the gaze draping the bed.

Alex.

Thinking her name sent a shaft of desire through him that mingled with relief so desperate it shivered his spine. Looking on her filled him with a sense of softness, begging him be gentle. He wanted to take her in his arms and carry her from that place and kiss every inch of her skin. She looked achingly innocent there, sleeping with one hand curled against her cheek, her hair spread around her in fine wisps. She was beautiful, at peace, and he wanted her with a suddenness that made his blood roil with frenzied passion.

He lifted the curtains aside, kneeling on the bed. She stirred, parting her lips on a sigh, unconsciously begging him to kiss her. The hour was late. He knew no one would disturb them. Who more than a guard could be up at the hour? He warred with himself, needing to make haste, but he had to kiss her as she lay, touch her with the gentleness he was capable of and had never shown her.

Losing the fight, Bronson eased onto the bed, lying beside her, looking down at her face, soft in the silvery light. He brushed a thumb across her lips, enjoying the feel of them. The were soft as rose petals. Unable to resist their velvet lure, he bent and touched his lips to hers, tasting her breath. 'Twas not enough—and never was.

He tugged her bottom lip, sucking it into his mouth, wanting to groan as he tasted how sweet she was—sweeter than he remembered. It seemed an eternity since he'd touched her. She moaned, coming awake, kissing him back, her tongue reaching out to him. He released her imprisoned lip, exchanging his captive for her tongue, sucking her into his mouth and mating his tongue with hers.

He reached a hand under the covers, down her belly and cupped her femininity through the night rail she wore, its sheerness no barrier to the heat between her legs, the instant moisture he aroused as he touched her. She whimpered into his mouth, parting her legs for him. Through the fragile fabric, he thrust his fingers into her core, his progress hampered by the cloth, frustrating them both.

He tore from her mouth, branding her neck with kisses, her broken sobs and arching body firing the need of his loins. He was hard with arousal, deaf to anything by her moans of pleasure.

"Do I dream?" she gasped, clutching the sheets as though he would tear her from them.

"Nay, wildcat," he breathed hot against her ear. "I came to steal you back."

She bit her lip as he moved his hand and thrust her rail aside, coming flush against her hot, wet flesh, toying with the bud that swelled against the pads of his fingers. She shivered, arching her neck as he tasted it and the gooseflesh that whispered across her skin.

His cock pushed against his cod piece, demanding freedom, seeking the molten sheath his fingers thrust into.

Her core clenched around him, nearing that peak that tantalized, quivering and unclenching. She cried out as he rasped her nub with his thumb, sucking a mark of possession beneath her ear.

"Bronson, pray," she breathed, frantically tugging his arm—, "give more, love. I need you inside me. I need … all … of … you."

He groaned raggedly, tearing his hand away to remove his cod piece.

A cold voice spoke behind him, halting his movement. "Take yer hand off yer sword, my lord, else I will do what my father could not."

Chapter Eighteen

Bronson sat up and shielded her from Kiara's eyes as she straightened herself. Alex looked around Bronson's massive shoulders as her cousin came fully into the room, leaving the door open behind her.

Kiara lit a candle in the sconce and regarded him angrily. Alex could see her temper was barely in check. Her hands were clenched tight, as though she would pummel Bronson, but in her right hand she held a sword—a broad sword—and she had every look of one who could use it.

Bronson stood, moving away from Alex. Alex swung her legs over the edge of the bed, dangling her feet, regarding her cousin with a mixture of horror, irritation, and gratitude.

"Yer a terrible thief, ye know. If you weren't so concerned on dipping yer wick, belswagger, you might have gotten away with it. As it is, I'm afraid I'll be forced to cut yer cods off. I've need of a lucky charm in these black days."

Alex choked, snorting, clamping her hands on her mouth as she looked back and forth between them. She expected any moment to see them come to blows. She could not identify which seemed the more determined to be victor.

Bronson frowned at the both of them. "How did you know I was here?" he demanded of Kiara.

"I've devilish keen ears, my lord. You would be amazed. Now, come with me else I'll be forced to throw you in the dungeon." She paused a long moment, and said, "Yer brothers await outside. 'Twas truly they who gave you away."

Bronson scowled, punching a fist into one palm as he walked toward Kiara.

"Father thought you damned Blackmores would try something. You canna blame yer brothers entirely. Men are too predictable by far," she said, pointing the sword at his back and prodding him out.

"Alex, you wait here while we deal with them. I trust you're okay?"

Alex nodded, still absorbed in the heat between her thighs and what Bronson had done. She watched them go, and shut the door behind them. Anger built, stagnating in her mind after they'd gone.

How dare that villain steal into her room, touch her as she slept, make her beg for his caresses. He was to wed another and still, he could not release his hold on her.

Alex shivered, ducking back into bed, huddling under the covers in pure misery. Her loins ached with need, conjured by that cocklorel. He thought of nothing but himself and his needs and wants. She despised him, and she despised her continued feeling of softness toward him.

She felt no conceit that he wanted her for herself, that his position had changed in the short time she'd been gone—it was only his immense vanity, his pride that made him come to her.

Despite the inflammatory reasons she told herself why she should hate him, she realized she did not. Her strength of will was weak. But it changed nothing.

He'd cast out her confidence of the McPherson castle. 'Twas not that she thought them lax, or its defenses incomplete, but she could not remain locked inside as a prisoner. She would have to go out, and she feared Bronson would be waiting for her.

She did not feel she could survive another encounter with him and still regain her sanity. Forbidden love held its own allure by its very nature, as addictive and intoxicating as heavy wine, but no less dangerous for her senses. Bronson was nothing less than the forbidden, a man untouchable, unattainable.

She had to remember that, no matter how much it hurt. On the morrow, she would ask her uncles to help her reach the king's court. She could not remain here. Bronson's actions tainted everything around her, until she saw and heard and smelled nothing but him.

Again, she was struck with the notion that he was some dread affliction. She shook her musings aside, settling into bed, the candle easing her fears as she closed her eyes.

Tomorrow, she would leave and never come back, for how could she stand to know that Bronson lived and loved with his new wife, so near to her.

* * * *

The Scotsmen 'escorted' the brothers to their horses and beyond, taking them to the borderlands. They'd appropriated their weapons, so they had no choice but to ride back home. There was naught more they could do.

Already the sky turned gray with the coming dawn. Bronson rode wearily, feeling as though some great weight settled on his neck, pressing him down into the saddle. They arrived at Derwin Hall, and he found that the household was awake, eager for news.

Bronson ignored them all, going inside and gathering a quantity of ale that he felt would make him forget all that had happened, and then staggered into the parlor to sit before the fire. He collapsed in the Glastonbury chair, spreading his legs straight out before him, draining his mug in one great swallow before he filled it again. He nursed his mug, staring into the flames, feeling a great emptiness gnawing inside him.

He heard the door open behind him, but he did not look to see who came, merely took another draught and wiped his mouth on his sleeve. The ale warmed the coldness gripping him, eased the tension of his body.

"I gather you did not succeed, son?" his father said quietly in his gruff voice, more a statement than a question.

"You mean I failed," Bronson said with a growl, finishing off his mug and pouring another.

His father pulled a chair beside him, laying his hand on his shoulder. Bronson shook his concern off, his black mood failing to dim.

"Drinking yourself into oblivion solves nothing," he said quietly.

"It makes me feel a hell of a lot better," he said angrily, taking a swallow for emphasis.

His father sighed heavily. "I would change your fate if I could. I had love once. I would have my sons happy in their marriage."

"I do not love her father," he said, turning bleak eyes to his father, his voice breaking with emotion. "She consumes me, mind, body, and soul for want of her honeyed thighs, but no more! 'Tis naught but a madness that seizes me in its vile grip."

He shook his head. "I understand."

"You do not. It is a sickness. One that needs purging. Leave me so that I might lance the wound," he roared.

His father stood, pushing the chair back from him, standing over him in quiet rage. "You gather the last of your wits, boy. You've fobbed off your bride too long as you dawdled with your bit of fluff. The Blackmores are men of their word. I will not have you break the honor of your lineage."

"I know my duty," Bronson said coldly.

"Good," his father responded, just as deadly cold. "You ride in a sennight."

* * * *

The days passed in a haze of intoxication. The eve before his departure, Gray and Rafael forced him from the parlor and toted him upstairs, dunking him into a tub of icy water fully clothed.

He came up sputtering, in a murderous rage, glaring at his brothers with blood in his eye. "I will kill you both," he swore, swiping his soaked hair back from his forehead—the better to see his targets.

"You have one last chance to see Alex before you depart, would you waste it with drink?" Gray asked in disgust, slapping the water and splashing Bronson with the frigid liquid.

Rafael regarded him with his arms across his chest, his face grim. They waited silently for his answer.

"What is your plan?" Bronson asked, grimly conceding he'd wallowed in misery for far too long.

"We go to see Hugh McPherson and ask for entrance ... as civilized men rather than thieves."

He nodded, recognizing his brothers' wisdom. He'd been unreasonable, worse than a pig, selfish to the point of destruction. Never had self-pity consumed him so unnaturally. He realized he had to thank his brothers for saving him from self-ruination, and he did. They nodded and left him, gone to prepare the horses.

Alone now, Bronson stripped his sodden garments off, flinging them to the floor in a wet heap. He bathed and washed the stink of liquor off his skin, shaving and dressing.

They were on their way by dusk. The landscape passed in a whirl, and before he comprehend it, they'd arrived at the McPhersons, had their arrival announced and were granted access inside. The McPhersons seemed to have graciously ignored his actions of before, for which he was grateful.

Hugh met them in the great hall, bidding them sit before the fire, offering them wine and ale. Bronson declined the comforts of drink, moving to the heart of his reason for coming. "Where is Alex? I must see her."

Hugh McPherson's smile faded, and he frowned, stroking the braids of his beard. He looked between the brothers, taking a sip of ale before he answered. "I thought mayhap you would come sooner, as our guests, but Alex refused to allow me to send word." He sighed, pausing for so long, it set Bronson's teeth on edge. "You'll not like this, lad. She is married, lad, and gone this past week."

An unseen hand punched his gut, knocking the breath from his lungs. He clutched his stomach with one arm, certain he would be ill, but the pain spread through him instead, changing to a numbness that burned with a cold as frigid as the deepest winter snow. "What?" he croaked, swallowing hard to moisten his mouth and throat.

He set his mug aside, giving Bronson a look of pity. "She is married, Lord Blackmore. There is naught you can do."

Hugh's words echoed in his ears, over and over again, taunting, driving his mind to split asunder.

Something died inside him.

He shook his head, getting to his feet, ignoring the stares and outbursts of the others. Pushing aside his brothers, he staggered out of that hellish hall, out into the cold bite of winter and the flakes of snow whirling down around him. There was nothing left for him now. No hope. Only emptiness and despair.

* * * *

Bronson rode with a fury to London, his family trailing behind him in slower conveyance. Now that he had nothing to stand in his way, he wanted to be done with this farce of a wedding and move on with his life.

The cold accentuated the bitterness permeating his soul, never failing to remind him that he continued to live. He could not bear to slow his pace, dangerous as it was. He hardly slept before he took to the rode again, didn't eat, only on the eve of his arrival did he stop to prepare himself to meet the king and his betrothed, though truthfully, he could care less of his appearance.

Within a week of hard riding, pushing both himself and his horse to the limits of endurance, he reached the city's outskirts, heading straight for the court. His family would find him—they knew where he went and his purpose.

For now, he would do what was required of him and mark the final seal on his fate—gaining the king's blessing for his nuptials.

Reaching his destination, Bronson handed Ebony to a stablehand, impatiently going through the motions of gaining admittance.

As he swept inside, his brother Nigel caught sight of him and left a group of men, intercepting him before he could proceed.

"Bronson!" he called, running up, clasping his brother in a warm hug, noting his brother's withdrawn air and impatience. "How fair you? We've expected you near a month now. Why were you delayed?"

Bronson's jaw hardened at the reminder of his failure. Would he never have peace? "'Tis none of your concern, brother. I go now to see the king."

Nigel frowned at him. "I will attend you. You've not the look of a well man, brother. I fear for your safety if you upset his highness."

Bronson grunted, not slowing his stride. He ignored the courtiers, the rich decadence of his surroundings, everything but his destination. Finally, he was upon it, access granted and ready to enter. The doors opened wide, he dimly heard his name announced as he strode up the center of the room and halted before his king.

The king sat on his throne, seeing to matters of state. He looked up at Bronson's entrance, mildly interested, but appearing more bored than anything else. Doubtless the cold confined him indoors.

Bronson knelt before him, bowing his head deeply, Nigel behind him in similar pose. "Your highness," he said, placing a hand on his heart as he knelt. "Long have I traveled to see you."

"Patience has never been a dominant feature, Lord Blackmore. Rise," King Henry VIII said, looking down at him, his brow wrinkled with a frown. "You come on the matter of your betrothal."

"Aye, I do," Bronson said, standing and assuming a respectful stance.

King Henry nodded and gestured to a servant with one hand. The silence in the room seemed to stretch abominably with anticipation. Bronson's blood roared in his ears as he waited.

The king made conversation with him, asking news on the borders of his kingdom, and it was all he could do to respond to the king's questions on the matter.

In a matter of minutes, struggling through the prolonged torture of conversing with royalty when he had no patience for it, Bronson heard the main door open behind them, and the king said, "She comes. Lord Bronson Blackmore, may I present, Lady Elizabeth Darrow."

Bronson turned stiffly, facing the woman he was to marry.

Alex stood in the center walkway, her eyes shining with tears, the fingertips of one hand pressed to her lips to hush her cries.

The steel glove gripped his heart, choked the breath out of him. He felt as if he'd been slapped in the face. "How can this be?" he whispered, unable to believe she stood before him, her hair unbound, clothed in a sumptuous emerald gown befitting royalty.

Alex ran to him, rushing into his arms. He closed her in his embrace, kissing her hair, her face with desperation, afraid he'd gone mad, that she would vanish from his arms. She kissed him back, ignoring the stares of the court, the presence of the king.

"You've met, I see," the king said behind them, a

smile in his voice. "There are chambers behind me if you care for privacy."

Without a word, they rushed to them, closing the door behind them. "What has happened?" Bronson asked on a ragged breath, unwilling to release her. "You are married—your uncle told me it was so."

She shook her head, kissing his face, cupping his jaw. "He misunderstood. He knew I was to be married as soon as I came here. I did not know the name of my groom until I arrived."

He gripped her shoulders, looking at her hard. "What is your name, Alex?"

"Elizabeth Alexandra Darrow. Montague was a lesser title of my father's. I took it when my grandfather died and I was forced to flee before the king could find me. All for naught. Had I but gone to the king as I should, I would have had you and been your wife even now."

He shuddered, closing her in his arms, shutting his eyes against the sting that pricked them. She squeezed him, sobbing against his chest.

"I thought I'd lost you," he whispered brokenly. "I … I died at the thought of you married to another. I journeyed here in a fog of pain, dying more and more each day that passed."

"I died too, thinking of you wedding another. I hated you, Bronson. Despised you for making me love you," she whispered.

He released her, cupping her chin and tilting her face up to his so that he could look into her eyes. "I love you, Alex," he murmured, descending for a kiss—, "Be my wife."

"Forever and always, my love," she whispered, meeting his kiss.

THE END